“You’re [illegible] bedroom with the balcony.”

Lilith stared at Tony. He saw her delicate jaw set, and knew he was going to have a fight on his hands. And he wasn’t in the mood. So instead of trying to persuade her with convincing arguments, he cut straight to the one he figured would win the quickest.

“You have two options,” he said evenly. “First, you sleep in the guest room without the balcony.”

She arched a brow at him. “Or?”

“Or you sleep in your bedroom, in your bed… with me.”

Dear Reader,

When I was writing the previous Redstone adventure, as sometimes happens, a secondary character began to creep in, demanding more and more face time. While this is always exciting, it's also annoying, because I find myself muttering, "This isn't your story, back off." (Yes, I talk to my characters. They talk to me, after all….)

But as anyone who read *Deadly Temptation* might guess, Tony Alvera wasn't about to go away completely, or quietly. And when my editor asked hopefully if he would have his own book—soon—I realized he'd just gone over my head. But not being one to go quietly myself, I decided to pay him back. I began to look around for the worst possible match for a tattooed, knife-wielding former street gangster. I found her in elegant, refined—and older—Lilith Mercer. And so the fun began.

I hope you will enjoy reading the tale of this mismatched yet meant-for-each-other couple as much as I enjoyed writing it.

Happy reading,

Justine Davis

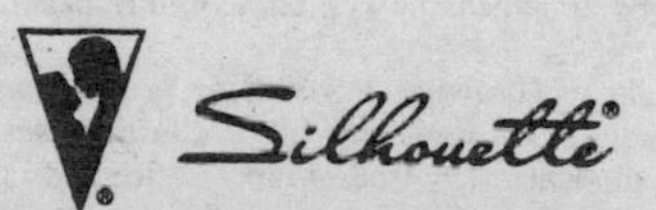

Romantic
SUSPENSE

Recycling programs for this product may not exist in your area.

ISBN-13: 978-0-373-27609-7
ISBN-10: 0-373-27609-5

BACKSTREET HERO

This edition published by arrangement with Harlequin Books S.A.

Visit Silhouette Books at www.eHarlequin.com

Printed in U.S.A.

Books by Justine Davis

Silhouette Romantic Suspense

Hunter's Way #371
Loose Ends #391
Stevie's Chase #402
Suspicion's Gate #423
Cool Under Fire #444
Race Against Time #474
To Hold an Eagle #497
Target of Opportunity #506
One Last Chance #517
Wicked Secrets #555
Left at the Altar #596
Out of the Dark #638
The Morning Side of Dawn #674
†*Lover Under Cover* #698
†*Leader of the Pack* #728
†*A Man to Trust* #805
†*Gage Butler's Reckoning* #841
†*Badge of Honor* #871
†*Clay Yeager's Redemption* #926
The Return of Luke McGuire #1036
**Just Another Day in Paradise* #1141
The Prince's Wedding #1190
**One of These Nights* #1201
**In His Sights* #1318
**Second-Chance Hero* #1351
**Dark Reunion* #1452
**Deadly Temptation* #1493
**Her Best Friend's Husband* #1525
**Backstreet Hero* #1539

†Trinity Street West
*Redstone, Incorporated

JUSTINE DAVIS

lives on Puget Sound in Washington. Her interests outside of writing are sailing, doing needlework, horseback riding and driving her restored 1967 Corvette roadster—with the top down, of course.

Justine says that years ago, during her career in law enforcement, a young man she worked with encouraged her to try for a promotion to a position that was at the time occupied only by men. "I succeeded, became wrapped up in my new job, and that man moved away, never, I thought, to be heard from again. Ten years later he appeared out of the woods of Washington state, saying he'd never forgotten me and would I please marry him. With that history, how could I write anything but romance?"

Chapter 1

It was, Lilith Mercer thought as she rubbed at her shoulder, her own fault. She hadn't been paying attention, and had walked right into some kid's practical joke. And had landed ungracefully on her backside.

"Are you sure you're all right?"

She smiled at her concerned neighbor. "Except for my bruised dignity, I'm fine."

"That was horrible," Mrs. Tilly said. She'd come rushing out at the no doubt embarrassingly loud thud Lilith had made hitting the landing outside her front door. "You could have fallen all the way down those stairs."

That fact hadn't escaped Lilith. If she hadn't managed to grab the stairway banister, the tumble down the concrete steps would have been ugly. Exiting her second-floor condo in a Monday morning rush with her hands full as usual, her mind already on the busy day ahead—also as usual—she hadn't seen the thin, silver wire strung tight across the top of the stairs.

"Lucky my reflexes are okay," she said, although to herself she was wondering just how sore the shoulder she'd wrenched in the process was going to be in a couple of days.

"It has to be that Wells boy," Mrs. Tilly said. "He's going to be the death of us all. The other day I saw him with a barbecue lighter, trying to start a fire on their patio."

Personally, Lilith found the apparent booby trap clearly intended to cause injury—if not worse—a bit more unsettling than a young boy's typical fascination with flames, but in Southern California, a state with a deadly yearly fire season, nothing to do with fire was taken lightly.

"It's a good thing you're a youngster and can bounce," Mrs. Tilly said grimly.

Lilith thought that at forty-four, she'd officially left being a youngster behind some time ago, but she supposed to her seventy-five-year-old neighbor that was a relative thing. And the implication was painfully true; had the older woman been the one to discover that wire the hard way, the results could have been horribly different.

"Someone needs to talk to Callie again," the woman said sternly.

The implication that, as usual, that someone should be her didn't escape Lilith. Martha Tilly hated confrontation and had decided—deservedly so, Lilith thought—that at her age avoiding it was her right. She didn't really mind; Mrs. Tilly was nothing if not blunt, sometimes to the point of rudeness, and Lilith wasn't sure that was the right approach with their downstairs neighbor. Especially just now.

"She has her hands full being a single mom with two kids, one of them a toddler," Lilith said. "I hate to pile more on her."

She also suspected, although she'd never spoken of it, that Callie had escaped the hands of an abusive husband, which put Lilith soundly on her side for more reasons than Mrs. Tilly knew.

"But that boy's getting out of hand," Mrs. Tilly said. "Why, you could have been killed!"

"I'll speak to her," Lilith promised, knowing that if she did, at least it wouldn't be a formal confrontation that would put the harried young woman on the defensive.

Reassured, Mrs. Tilly at last let her continue on her way, although not without a promise to give young Billy Wells a piece of her mind if she saw him.

As she got into her car, Lilith felt a little tug in her shoulder, and, she noted ruefully, a spot on her backside that she was sure would be sore by tomorrow. She might well spend tomorrow working on her feet, she thought.

By the time she got to her office in the Research and Development division of Redstone Inc., she'd almost forgotten the incident. The huge task that still lay before her took her full concentration, and her determination to fix this situation for Josh Redstone demanded she give it just that. That Josh of all people, the most generous and loyal man she'd ever known, had been the victim of industrial spying rankled her beyond belief. She would find every last detail of what had happened and salvage everything that could be salvaged, no matter how long it took.

She sat down at her desk—a U-shaped arrangement that was more functional than decorative—and booted up her computer, still feeling the surge of energy that hit her every day when she arrived at Redstone Headquarters. She had a very proprietary feeling about Redstone, and about its brilliant founder, Joshua Redstone. She'd known him for better than twenty-five years now, and he had soared past even her own stellar predictions for his future.

As an eighteen-year-old teacher's aide, she hadn't been fooled by the languid drawl; even at fifteen the intelligence in those gray eyes had fairly snapped at her. She'd guessed early on that the air some mistook for laziness was merely boredom with a curriculum that didn't challenge him, and she'd taken it upon herself to provide that challenge, guiding him toward more advanced work that he could undertake on his own.

And eventually, toward getting his G.E.D. and getting out before his seventeenth birthday; he was already so far beyond high school she didn't think he'd survive two more years, and was only where he was because his small family—himself, his father and his older brother—had moved around a lot.

At first he'd been suspicious—neither did that drawl mean he was a fool, as many had learned along the way, to their detriment—but she'd kept on, until he rose to the bait. She'd had the feeling he'd known exactly what she was doing, but had let her lead him. And then, after he'd easily passed the G.E.D. tests and she'd told him exactly how far she thought he could go, he'd made her a promise. She'd been the first person other than his brother to really believe in him, he'd said. Someday he'd repay her.

He certainly had.

"What's wrong, Lilith?"

Only when she heard the voice of her assistant, Liana Kiley, did she realize she'd been rubbing her shoulder again. She looked up at the young woman and ruefully explained.

"A wire?" Liana stared at her, eyes wide. "You could have been seriously hurt. Or worse."

"So my neighbor informed me," Lilith said. "But the only damage was a scrape on my briefcase, and sore spots in my shoulder and...landing zone."

That got her a smile, but Liana's concern didn't abate. It was one of the first traits Lilith had noticed about the bright, lovely redhead; she had a large capacity for compassion, a trait that made her an excellent fit for Redstone.

It had also netted Liana the man in her life, new Redstone Security team member Logan Beck. Liana's concern for the ex-cop who had once saved her life had not only gotten him out of a morass of injustice, it had opened up a new life for both of them, together.

"And it was only last Thursday that truck nearly hit you. You could have been killed."

Lilith smiled to reassure Liana. "Let's hope it's not going to be a string of bad luck."

Liana frowned. Lilith knew that look. Liana had worn it often enough in her first days here, when Logan had been struggling against false accusations of being a crooked cop.

But they'd come through it and become yet another of the growing list of couples brought together under the Redstone banner. Lilith found it amusing as well as bemusing that so many soul mates had found each other through Redstone. She'd teased Josh once about his heretofore unknown matchmaking talent, but she actually tended to believe longtime Redstone pilot Tess Machado's more pragmatic explanation when you brought smart, talented people with the same principles and standards together, as Redstone did, it was only to be expected.

"Let's get going," she said briskly, knowing Liana would accept that as a diversion; even now she was still feeling a bit guilty that her first days on the job had been taken up completely by her quest for justice for Logan. Even though Lilith had assured her she'd more than made up for it in the months since, the young woman she'd come to genuinely like would never take Redstone for granted, not after what they'd done for her and Logan.

About an hour later, Lilith had just hung up from a conversation with Redstone's resident genius inventor, Ian Gamble, the man whose work had been the target of the industrial spying that had blown up into the scandal that had destroyed the JetCal Corporation and sent both their CEO and Redstone R&D head Stan Chilton to prison, when Josh himself appeared in her doorway.

While it was a tradition for Redstone's leader to make a tour of his headquarters any day he was present, he usually came by earlier in the day. It was common knowledge to all Redstone people that this was their chance to ask him anything, as Liana had learned; a casual mention had resulted in the mobilization of Redstone's much vaunted private security team and the vindication of Logan Beck.

"Running late?" Lilith said with a smile.

Josh didn't smile back. His gray eyes fastened on her intently as he came into the office. And he didn't stroll, in that loose-limbed, lanky way he had, he strode in like the head of a multinational conglomerate that he was.

Instinctively responding to the difference, Lilith stood, wondering with some trepidation what was wrong. "Josh?"

He just stood there for a moment, looking her up and down. She knew better than to think he disapproved of her casual attire; jeans and the red knit shirt with the Redstone logo were the unofficial uniform for many of Redstone's people, and she'd been glad she'd had the tough denim on when she'd hit the concrete this morning.

The moment the thought came into her mind, her puzzlement vanished and Josh's demeanor and actions made sense.

"Liana, I presume?" she said ruefully; she should have known the girl wouldn't keep this to herself.

"Logan."

"I'm fine, Josh."

He looked her up and down once more. She held up her arms to display she was unhurt. "See? Nothing broken, snapped or otherwise seriously impaired."

He didn't look convinced.

"Repeat after me," she said, in her best teacher's voice, "'You look fine, Lilith.'"

At last he eased up. "You look…elegant, as usual, even in blue jeans, Lilith."

She laughed. This was old ground between old friends as

well; he teased her about what he called her refined air and elegant grace, so opposite of his own down-home, laid-back demeanor. Hers, he had once said, masked a steely spine, boundless energy and whip-smart intelligence. She had simply looked at him, and in a deadly accurate imitation of his own lazy drawl, had said, "Back at you."

"You know," he said now, with a casualness that warned her he was anything but, "I don't believe in coincidences. Not when it comes to danger to my people."

Lilith's brows rose. "Danger?"

"Two narrow escapes in a week?"

She chuckled. "That sounds so dramatic. I nearly had a traffic accident. And this morning I ran afoul of a child's prank."

"Maybe."

"Coincidence, Josh."

"You know what Draven says about coincidence."

"Draven," she said, "is a born cynic." Then remembering how the Redstone Security chief had mellowed since his marriage to Grace O'Conner, she added, "At least, he was when he always used to say that."

"And now he's more protective than ever. So when I tell him about this, he's going to take appropriate action."

"Tell him? Why on earth?"

"Because I don't believe in coincidence, either. Not when one of my brightest and best has uncharacteristic 'accidents.'"

"Thank you for the compliment, but really—"

Josh stopped her with an upheld hand. "No compliment, just truth. As is the fact that you're going to have to tolerate a little attention for a while, until I'm sure this doesn't mean anything."

"Mean anything? You mean like someone's intentionally trying to hurt me?"

She started to laugh even before she finished the words, but when Josh simply looked at her, his jaw set, realization struck and her laughter faded away.

"Yes," he finally said, his voice echoing with grim acknowledgment of what they both knew but she had managed to put out of her mind.

There indeed was someone who could be trying to hurt her. Or even kill her.

Because he'd tried it before.

Chapter 2

Tony Alvera didn't stop to knock on his boss's door, any more than he had bothered to park his racy blue coupe in an allotted slot; he was in too much of a hurry. He knew he'd committed a breach of decorum when he realized John Draven was with someone in his small, efficiently organized office, but there were times when he reverted to his younger days of not caring about such things, and this was one of them.

"Sorry," he said perfunctorily, nodding at the woman in the office.

Because he wasn't really sorry, there wasn't much sincerity in the apology, and Draven lifted a brow at him. Since it was the one already slightly twisted by the scar that slashed down the left side of his face, the look was even more intimidating.

But Tony Alvera wasn't a man who was easily intimidated.

"I need to talk to you," he said.

"Taylor Hill," Draven said mildly, "meet Tony Alvera. Pay

attention, you may have to work with him someday. I hear it's an adventure."

Tony had heard that Draven was bringing in someone new, to fill in now that Samantha Gamble, married to Redstone's resident genius, Ian Gamble, was visibly pregnant. Sam might grumble about being tied to a desk, but her work instincts were trumped by newfound maternal ones, and she'd ruefully agreed that going into the field on assignments that could turn risky was not in her best interest just now.

For a moment Tony thought of Ian, that brilliant, creative mind that had put Redstone on the map in so many new fields that not even Josh could keep track of them all. As had most at Redstone, Tony had marveled from the beginning at the unlikelihood of Ian and Sam's relationship—the man some teasingly called the absentminded professor and the stunning, leggy blonde.

He'd been even more bemused by the easy way Ian seemed to accept the differences between them, accept Sam's sometimes dangerous job and the fact that she was one of the best at it. He often joked he was the brains while his wife was the brawn with brains. Tony wasn't sure he could so blithely accept his woman working in a traditionally masculine role.

At the same time, he utterly and totally respected Samantha Gamble and her skills and would gladly have her at his back in any tough situation. The conflict niggled at him, but he didn't dwell on it much, preferring to see it as a hangover from days past that he tried not to think about. When he did think about them, it was usually with a rueful jab at himself and the street gang culture of machismo he'd grown up in.

The woman in the office was standing now, studying him less than subtly as she held out a hand. He took it—her grip was solid but not overly so—and automatically assessed her in turn, a habit ingrained in him during his years with Redstone Security.

Taylor Hill was an ordinary-looking woman, with straight, medium brown hair pulled back rather severely at the nape of her neck. She was average height and build, her features regular but not striking. She was neither unattractive nor beautiful, but fell in the unremarkable category.

The perfect person for security work, Tony thought. She could probably blend in anywhere.

"Nice to meet you," she said politely, and his opinion suddenly changed. That low, husky voice would stand out in any man's mind. And make him wonder, if she sounded like that now, what she might sound like in more intimate circumstances.

But he had no time for speculating about other women at the moment.

"You, too," he replied, aware it was a disconnected nicety but unable to help it.

"I was about to send Taylor off on her first assignment," Draven said in a casually chatty manner completely unlike him. "Nothing like starting out doing a favor for Josh himself."

That snapped Tony to attention. Was there something else going on at Redstone besides what he'd come here about? "Josh has a problem?"

"One of his people has a problem, so yes, you could say that."

Tony felt the adrenaline spurt ebb a little. He looked his boss in the eye, a task more easily said than done to almost anyone who had to deal with the steely, tough John Draven.

"Lilith," he said.

Draven's brow rose again. "You know?"

"Beck," he said briefly, knowing that would explain; Logan Beck, the newest—well, now apparently second newest—member of the security team, was engaged to Liana Kiley, Lilith Mercer's assistant.

He was also Tony's partner in situations that required a two-man team; they'd worked well together on Logan's case, and although he generally preferred to work alone—as did Logan—Tony was now amenable to the pairing when necessary.

"I'll handle it," Tony said.

Draven lifted a brow. "What?"

"This one's mine." At Draven's expression, Tony turned back to Taylor, who was watching this exchange curiously. "Would you excuse us for a minute, please?"

The woman's glance flicked to Draven, who, after a split second, gave her a barely perceptible nod. She didn't miss the signal and left without a word.

"She's going to be good," Draven said when Tony didn't speak right away.

"Yeah," Tony muttered.

He began to pace the small room. Now that he was here and had his boss's attention, he had no idea what to say. He should, he realized, have thought about this a little more before he'd burst in.

He should have thought about it a little more, period, he thought. Had he learned nothing from Lisa? Had he forgotten standing in the morgue, looking down at her lifeless body, knowing she was there because of him?

I'm trying to stop something like that from happening again, he told himself as Draven continued to speak of the woman who had just left.

"She did some good work at Redstone in Toronto. She was ready to move up."

"Yeah."

Silence seemed to echo in the room while Tony continued to pace and tried to figure out what to say.

"You got back last night?"

"Yeah."

He left it at that. The Hawk IV that had picked him up in Caracas had actually touched down a little after 1:00 a.m., so technically this morning, but he knew Draven already knew that. And he'd already filed his report in flight, so he knew Draven knew the final result of his investigation into the local kickback problem as well.

"You know," Draven said at last, "I'm told I talk more than I used to these days, but I'm in no way comfortable carrying on a whole conversation myself. What do you want, Alvera?"

Tony stopped mid-stride and spun around to face his boss. "I want this job." There, he thought. It was out.

"What job?"

"The one you were going to give her," he said, jerking a thumb toward the door where Taylor had exited.

Draven frowned. "I don't think this is anything that requires your…unique skills, Tony."

"Nothing does, at the moment."

Not really his decision to make, but he knew it was true. Lucky for him, Draven was in a flexible mood this morning.

"There may not even be a real problem," his boss said. "It could just be a fluke, coincidence. Accidents and pranks do happen."

Not to Lilith, Tony thought.

"It's probably nothing, but Josh wants to be sure," Draven said. "You know how he is about his people."

"Yes. I do."

No one knew better than he did about Josh Redstone. Tony doubted there was another man on the planet who would have done what Josh did after an angry, scared, knife-wielding gang-banger had tried to mug him outside an L.A. hotel. Tony hadn't even realized he was trying to rob the wunderkind whose Redstone Aviation was beginning to soar, had seen only a man headed toward a limo, which to him had meant money and made the man a target.

He hadn't expected that the man would fight back, and well enough to have his sixteen-year-old ass on the pavement in less than ten seconds.

And he never would have dreamed that that man, not even ten years older than he himself, would see something in that angry kid, something that, instead of calling the cops as he should have, made him give Tony the chance of a lifetime. The chance at a life.

A life he would always owe to Josh Redstone.

"This is probably nothing a couple of days of simple investigation can't close," Draven said, looking at him with growing curiosity, the last thing Tony wanted.

"Then I won't be tied up long," he said, more sharply than he liked.

Draven's mouth quirked slightly. "You really want this?"

"I want this. Sir," he added, not caring that it was so obviously an afterthought tacked on to ameliorate the gruffness of his prior words.

Draven's brows lowered even farther. "You don't look—or sound—too sure about that."

Leave it to Draven to see past the surface, because truth be told, he wasn't. In fact, he was reasonably sure he would regret it; it was only the extent of that regret he wasn't sure of right now. But that didn't seem to make any difference.

"I mean it," he insisted.

Draven studied Tony for a long, silent moment. Tony set his jaw and waited, knowing Draven wasn't a man to be pushed.

"Why?" Draven finally asked.

Tony had prepared for that question, at least. "You know I worked with her a lot, during Beck's case. We…got along. I'd like to help, and I'm free, with nothing on the horizon that would require me more than anyone else on the team."

Draven listened, looking thoughtful. If he noticed that this prosaic explanation was at odds with the inner tension Tony was feeling—and Tony had little doubt Draven would sense that, there was very little that escaped him—he didn't comment on the fact.

Just when Tony thought he'd blown it, and that Draven, with that preternatural instinct of his, had somehow guessed the secret Tony Alvera kept hidden from everyone, his boss slowly nodded.

"All right. But if something in your area comes up—"

"I understand," Tony said, barely aware of interrupting the

legendary head of Redstone Security, something few dared to do. Or had the chance to do; as he'd said, Draven wasn't known for talking a lot.

The size of the relief that flooded Tony at actually getting the assignment set off alarms clanging in the back of his head, but he was too thankful to pay them much heed.

A few minutes later he was back outside the airport hangar that served as operations for Redstone Security. They had always been housed off-site, keeping a low profile away from headquarters for the most part, a strategy that paid off on those rare occasions when a Redstone operative needed to go unrecognized. Plus, the airport location made quick response times easier, when some far-flung part of the Redstone empire needed their attention.

So you've got the job, he thought as he got into his car. Now what?

He had no answer. He told himself he should simply proceed as if this were any other job. Redstone Security had a reputation for efficiency, speed and success; all he had to do was live up to that. All he had to do was keep Lilith Mercer safe. No problem.

Never mind that he'd just volunteered to walk into a personal minefield.

He was so going to regret this. But he had to do it. He couldn't let anyone else take the job. Not this job. Because nobody else had a bigger stake in this than he did. Nobody else in Redstone Security was in his unique position.

Hell, nobody else would believe he was *in* this position.

Nobody would ever believe that onetime L.A. gang member, repeat juvenile offender, street-tough, tattooed Tony Alvera had been half in love with the elegant, classy, refined, beautiful and near-perfect Lilith Mercer since the first time he'd laid eyes on her.

No, no problem at all.

Chapter 3

Lilith felt absurd, but it was clear to her that Josh wasn't going to back down. And when Josh Redstone was set on something, it would take more than a mere protest to shift him. Besides, with what she owed him, she would tolerate a lot worse than having someone from security hanging around to placate his fears, however unfounded they might be.

Might, she thought, being the operative word.

Because once she'd read the thoughts in Josh's steady gray eyes, she'd realized she couldn't say with one hundred percent certainty that there was no one who would want to hurt her.

"Are you angry with me?"

The quiet question from her office doorway interrupted Lilith's unsettling thoughts. She looked up, into Liana Kiley's troubled blue eyes.

"No," she said to the young woman who had rapidly become indispensable to her in the task of finding and assessing the damage done by Stan Chilton, and had in the process become a friend as well. "I'm not angry. It's all right, Liana."

"I couldn't help worrying, and Logan agreed. I know the people who did this—" the redhead made a general gesture toward the research lab "—are in jail, but still..."

Lilith masked her start of surprise. That possibility hadn't occurred to her. She'd assumed, as had Josh, that if there was indeed some nefarious plot to harm her, only one person could be behind it. Of course, Liana didn't know about that person. No one did, except Josh, and at his request, security chief John Draven.

If she had to accept that something was really happening, she wished she could believe it was something as sanitary as fallout from the industrial spying case. That would be preferable to the alternative. But the alternative, unhappily, made a lot more sense.

"Thank you for being worried," Lilith said. "Although I don't think it's necessary."

"Logan thought it was better to be sure. You're not upset that he said something to Josh?"

"I wish he would have talked to me first, I could have eased his mind—and yours—but I try not to get angry with people who care enough to worry about me."

Liana smiled in obvious relief. "What's Josh going to do?"

"Pester me, no doubt," Lilith said, with fond annoyance. "Or rather, some unlucky person from security who no doubt has much more important things to do than find a plot where there is none will get that job."

"A bodyguard?"

Lilith laughed. "Oh, please. That's the last thing I need."

"They do that, though, don't they? Security, I mean? Because Logan would be happy to—"

She stopped when Lilith held up a hand. "I do *not* need a bodyguard."

A sudden image flashed through her mind, of the aftermath

of the last time a Redstone Security agent had taken on bodyguard duties. In her mind she saw Ian Gamble, dressed in a sleek tuxedo that erased any memory of his usual, casually untidy self, just as his intense expression as he waited for his beautiful bride had erased the memory of his usual, endearingly distracted self.

Ian Gamble, genius inventor, who had fallen in love and married Samantha Beckett, top-notch Redstone Security agent.

His bodyguard.

Yet another in the ongoing string of Redstone weddings.

She shook off the image briskly. "I'm sure he'll simply have someone look into both incidents, discover they were indeed unfortunate accidents and we will all go on about our business. Which is," she added, "what I intend to do now."

"Not just yet."

The deep voice from the doorway spun Liana around and made Lilith's nerves jump. Liana greeted the man standing there with a happy exclamation. "Tony! When did you get back?"

Lilith just tried to remember how to breathe.

"Hello, my lovely Liana. This morning," Tony said.

"Have you seen Logan?"

"Your knight in shining armor with the luck of a thousand men to end up with you? No, but I spoke to him, also this morning."

Liana laughed. "You're incorrigible. But that's what I love about you."

Lilith smiled to herself a little wistfully; the teasing repartee was so carefree. Tony Alvera was an incurable flirt, and Liana obviously knew it. Although even if he had been serious, it wouldn't have made any difference; the girl was head over heels in love with her ex-cop.

Lilith wondered if Tony Alvera was ever serious when it came to women. She was reasonably sure, from what she'd observed during his work on Logan's case, that he would never poach on another man's territory. Or perhaps that only applied to men he respected, as she knew he did Logan Beck. In any case, Liana was as safe from his predatory charms as if she'd been his sister. That, Lilith was certain of.

"But alas," Tony was saying with mock drama, "as always, I am too late to win the fair lady."

Lilith at last found her voice, and her poise.

"Children, children," she said in mock severity, "take the bantering outside, please. I have work to do."

Liana laughed, patted Tony's arm in a way that put her previous words clearly into that sisterly category and went back to her own office.

Tony Alvera didn't move. And at Lilith's teasing words or tone, something had flickered in his eyes that had caught her attention. Something that reminded her that for all his easy, practiced charm, this was a dangerous man.

Something you shouldn't forget, she told herself, although she wasn't sure why it seemed so important at this moment; since they were both Redstone, he would never be dangerous to her.

For a long moment he stood there, just looking at her. He wasn't a huge man, just under six feet she guessed, but he somehow managed to fill the room anyway. It must be the combination of obvious strength, the striking looks, dark eyes coupled with golden skin and the rather rakish patch of beard below the middle of his lower lip, and the edginess he radiated at almost every moment.

The evidence that the edginess was for real was clear in the barely noticeable patches of slightly lighter skin on his neck and hands, where she knew gang tattoos had once been.

When she'd first met him, when he'd been assigned to help Liana and Logan, she'd found him disconcerting, to say the least. When she'd learned his story, from Josh himself, she'd found him admirable.

Right now, standing solidly in her office staring at her a little too intently—and for some reason apparently not willing to leave as Liana had—he was nothing less than unsettling.

And suddenly the obvious answer hit her.

"Not you," she said, nearly groaning it.

His face changed. The transfixing look vanished, replaced by the practiced charm she'd seen him use so effectively before. Not the teasingly flirtatious manner he'd had with Liana; that had been oddly innocent and sincere. This was the demeanor he used to beguile people, mostly women, she was certain, into giving him what he wanted.

Whatever that might be.

That was something that hit a chord deep within her, and not in a good way.

"Sorry, Mrs. Mercer. Luck of the draw."

She was hideously aware that she'd uttered her gut reaction aloud. And since she wasn't even sure what had prompted that reaction, she didn't know quite how to explain it to herself, let alone to the man she'd just unintentionally insulted.

But manners dictated she say something, so she opted for simplicity. And truth, which was never an optional choice for her, not anymore. "I'm sorry. I'm just not sold on this whole idea, and it seems absurd to pull you, of all people, in on such a silly little thing."

And that was all true, she told herself. It just wasn't all of the truth. There had been something much more deeply rooted in that involuntary response to his presence. It wasn't that he wasn't efficient and effective—he wouldn't have lasted in Redstone Security if he wasn't And she had admired how he'd handled Logan's case, including how he'd dealt with the stubborn, reluctant ex-cop. But that contact had been intermittent. She couldn't imagine having to deal with his intense presence all the time.

His expression changed again, but only slightly. After a moment he nodded, as if in acceptance of her explanation. But the original, riveting stare didn't return, and somehow that unsettled her even more. Why, she didn't know. She was usually unruffled and ever calm; it was the trait most commented on by anyone who knew her. But now—

"We need to talk about what's happened. Who might want you hurt. I'll try not to disrupt your life too much. But this is on Josh's orders, and you know what that means."

"I know it means anyone at Redstone would walk through fire if he asked, yes."

"Even if he didn't ask," Tony said. "Because he wouldn't."

"He wouldn't have to," Lilith said, thinking of her own debt to the man who had built this empire.

"No," Tony agreed.

This, at least, they had in common, she thought. They would both do anything for Josh Redstone. She knew why Tony would; his story was legend at Redstone, along with Draven's and Ian's and many others.

And it suddenly hit her that she was going to have to tell him her own story. And that made her feel faintly nauseated.

If only Samantha wasn't pregnant. She could have told her, much more easily. She doubted the tough, beautiful blonde could have related—she doubted Samantha Gamble had ever been truly afraid in her life—but she would have understood.

The moment the thought formed she was appalled at herself; Samantha and Ian were delighted, if bemused, at their impending parenthood, and to wish that away, even for a split second, for her own benefit made Lilith ashamed of herself.

It was time to get a grip.

"Close the door, would you, please? The fewer people who know about this, the happier I'll be."

Tony complied without a word. Lilith walked back to her desk and sat down. Normally she would have taken the second chair in front of her desk, but she needed the bulwark.

Because she had just shut herself into a small room with the one person at Redstone who made her unbearably nervous.

It was going to be a very long morning.

Chapter 4

Just when did you become a masochist?

As he sat in the chair opposite her desk, relieved now that he'd seen for himself that she indeed seemed uninjured, he was very aware that she'd chosen to take her desk chair for the feeling of power or security it gave her, and the benefit of the desk between them. He also knew the answer to his own question. The moment he'd realized Josh was convinced Lilith could really be in some kind of danger, he'd had no choice. Even knowing he was going to regret it.

He already did.

The moment he'd walked in and seen her, all the truths he'd lived with since he'd first met her had risen up to swamp him anew. Lilith Mercer was everything he was not: elegant, refined, classy, cultured. He knew, thanks to the world Josh had opened to him, that he could put on the appearance of all those things. But he also knew that in him they were only skin deep. In Lilith, they went clear to the bone.

And he hadn't missed her reaction when she'd seen him; she didn't want him around. It puzzled him for a moment; they had gotten along well enough during his work on Logan's case, when she had asked him to keep her posted for Liana's sake.

But this was different, he supposed. This was her own situation, and because of that the contact would be much closer. He probably seemed like some kind of alien being to her, and he couldn't blame her. He knew who and what he was, and all the polish he'd acquired since his days on the street couldn't change that. His world and hers couldn't be further apart.

That hadn't stopped him from falling like a fool the moment he'd first seen her at the Redstone Christmas party, after Josh had called her in to clean up Stan Chilton's mess. He knew the image of her in that striking red dress would be with him until he died. Somehow the red had startled him; she seemed so reserved, but someone—he couldn't remember who, just as he couldn't remember much of what had happened that night after he'd seen her—had told him it was her favorite color and she wore it often.

He could see why; today she had on the Redstone logo shirt in a more muted shade, and it still set off her hair like golden fire.

He stared at her, all the warnings he'd given himself on the way over lost in some kind of hot haze. If there was anything more absurd or impossible in his life than such a reaction to her, of all women, he couldn't think of what it was. Not only was she all those things he wasn't, but she was a Redstone department head and one of Josh's oldest friends. That she was likely a bit older than he was didn't bother him, but all the rest did. He owed his very life to Josh, and he would never forget that.

And if that doesn't work, he told himself in an effort to clear the fog, just remember the last time you felt anything like this for a woman.

That memory—the image of a lovely, lifeless body lying on a cold metal table—managed what nothing else had. The last time he'd let himself truly feel something for a woman, it had gotten her murdered.

Back in control now, his rioting senses jammed back into the cage where they belonged, he repeated his promise. "I know this is a nuisance for you. I'll try to keep out of your way."

"I am sorry," she said, and she sounded more genuine this time. "I didn't mean to react that way. But this is a bit…below your talents."

"Some of them," he said, quashing the thought of other talents he'd like to exercise with her, shoving that cage door shut. "But I'm here, free at the moment, and we're not…strangers."

"No," she agreed. "And you know I was very impressed with what you did on Logan's case. I know he was… difficult, at that point in his life."

Tony chuckled, feeling a bit easier now. And pleased with her praise, he admitted ruefully. "Difficult? Yes, like a croc with a toothache is difficult."

When she laughed in turn, he felt an odd sense of gratification that his rather lame joke had done it. He shoved a little harder on that cage door.

"I just don't think this is anything serious. I'm not sure it's anything at all."

"Then it should be quick," he said smoothly, determined now to approach the job as if it were any other in-house assignment. "I'll need to see where that wire was rigged. And talk to the kid your neighbor suspects. But for now, why don't you tell me why Josh is convinced that you're in continuing danger?"

She looked puzzled. "He didn't tell you? Didn't Draven?"

"I wanted you to tell me. One less filter to go through."

She lifted one shoulder, somehow making even that half shrug seem elegant. "He has some idea my near-accident last week and what happened this morning are connected, I presume." She met his gaze then. "He did tell you that much? What happened?"

Tony nodded. "He said you weren't hurt. Is that true, or were you trying to keep him from worrying?"

"If I was, I obviously didn't succeed," she said, her dry tone making him smile in spite of himself.

"Josh is a hard sell when it comes to the welfare of his people."

"How well I know," she agreed, at last giving him that smile that could warm a room, the smile that encompassed everything, that drew him to her so impossibly; warmth, charm, grace and the generous spirit that had quickly made her one of the most loved Redstone people. That the smile wasn't really for him, but rather for the absent Josh, didn't lessen the impact.

"I'm fine," she said in answer to his original question. "No serious damage except to my pride and my derriere."

And a fine one it is.

The thought formed before he could stop it. Although she generally dressed fairly conservatively, her fire and flair coming in the frequent splashes of her favorite red, when she wore jeans as she did today, there was no disguising the fineness he'd just thought about.

Hell, he thought about it every time he saw her, and that alone made him aware of how out of line he was. He couldn't imagine any other man at Redstone having raunchy, lustful thoughts about Lilith Mercer. Longing, aching, desire, yes, but not the kind of urgent, desperate craving she made him feel.

That everyone at Redstone seemed to think he had a harem of women at his beck and call only made the irony bite deeper. He couldn't deny that there were women. And although he'd long ago quit trying to analyze why the combination of his looks and demeanor had a rather astonishing effect on some, he couldn't deny the fact, either.

Nor could he deny that he did, on occasion, use that fact. The only thing he tried to deny, to himself, was how meaningless it all was. What had once seemed like a dream come true, had become...he wasn't sure what. While if necessary he still turned on the charm to get what he needed, be it information or entrée to somewhere he normally couldn't get into, the instances where he pursued the connection to the inevitable destination—a willing woman's bed—had become few and far between.

He wasn't sure exactly why. He just didn't seem to have the energy or the desire to continue the facade anymore. He'd wondered if something was wrong with him, if he'd somehow lost the ability to feel any real desire.

Then he'd met Lilith Mercer. And the ferocious kick in the gut and points south had disabused him of that idea forever.

And forever was about how long he'd have to wait for the likes of Lilith Mercer to have a corresponding response to the likes of him.

He gave a final, hard shove to thoughts and urges that had no place here, and this time he locked the damned cage door.

"Tell me," he said, sounding gruffer than he'd intended. Keeping a leash on his unruly thoughts was proving harder than he'd expected.

Lilith sighed. Lowered her gaze to her hands. That alone had him sitting up straighter; of the myriad things he'd noticed about her since he'd met her, one was that she never avoided, never shrank from any difficult situation. As Josh said, she met it head-on and always gave it her best shot.

And her best shot, Josh had added, was very good indeed.

But she was avoiding looking at him now. He knew better than to think it was anything to do with him. It was something to do with this situation, and his gut was telling him that maybe Josh was right. Maybe there was more to this than just a couple of accidents.

His gut wasn't liking that idea. At all.

And she still wasn't talking.

"Stan Chilton's in jail," he said, managing a calmer tone this time. "And so is Joe Santerelli, from JetCal. Not to mention the fact that all you've done is come in to clean up the mess they caused. You didn't have anything to do with putting them there."

She still didn't look at him. But she answered. "I put together a lot of the data evidence that helped put them away."

She'd said it, but Tony sensed she didn't truly believe it. "True enough," he said, and waited.

"But if they wanted revenge, wouldn't they go after Draven? Or Sam and Ian?"

"Didn't work out so well for them last time, going up against those two."

At the mention of the unlikeliest couple at Redstone a trace of a smile curved her mouth.

That luscious mouth he couldn't keep his eyes off.

¡Maldita sea!

He knew when he resorted to his native Spanish that he was in trouble. And damning everything at large seemed to require that.

"You don't think it has anything to do with the spying case, do you?"

The smile faded. He regretted that, but this was more important.

"No," she said, in a tone of voice he could never have imagined coming from her. Weary, hurt, broken…he wasn't sure what it was, only that he didn't like it. Not from her.

"Then what? Or should I ask, who?"

Finally, she looked at him. Her usually bright blue eyes were shadowed now. Haunted, in a way he'd seen only in people in trouble, or in people from his days on the streets.

"Lilith," he said softly, aware but unable to stop himself from removing the safe barrier of formality of last name only.

"Daniel Huntington." She took a deep breath. "My ex-husband."

He blinked. He'd known she'd been married, but also that it

had ended before she'd come to Redstone. Long enough ago that it hadn't concerned him. Realizing he'd been glad to learn that had been his first clue that he was slipping into dangerous territory.

His brow furrowed. "I thought… Then why 'Mrs.' Mercer if it's your maiden name?"

"I dropped his name. People assumed the Mrs. because they knew I'd been married, and it was just…easier."

And kept men away? he wondered. Not that it would keep some away, but the some it wouldn't deter would be the kind she wouldn't be interested in anyway. He knew that much already.

"What about him?" he asked.

"Josh suspects that if these things are more than accidents…he might be behind it."

"Why would he think that?"

"Past history. But it's as impossible that it's him as it is that it's Stan Chilton or Santerelli."

He could see that she didn't want to get into it, so although he knew they'd have to talk about it eventually, he changed tacks. "Where is he? Local?"

"That depends," she said, finally giving him the level look that was her norm, "on whether you consider Chino local."

He shrugged off the first thought that hit him; half the kids he'd grown up with were in Chino. At the California Institute for Men. But there was no way…

His thoughts faded as the way she was looking at him slowly registered.

"Yes," she said, that weariness he'd heard before echoing in her voice again.

"He's…in prison?"

"Has been for nearly two years."

He was beyond puzzled. The only thing he could think of was that the man had committed some white-collar crime.

"He's on the Level I side? Minimum security?" he asked, although he didn't understand why the man wasn't in some country club kind of place instead of a hard-core lockup like Chino. Guys from *his* world went to Chino. Not hers.

"No. Medium security."

Belatedly it hit him. If Josh suspected her ex might be behind what had been happening to her, then he must have a reason.

"What is he in for?"

She held his gaze with that nerve that had only wavered for a moment. "He tried to kill me."

Chapter 5

She'd seen that look before. The shock, the incredulity. It was nothing new to her, that kind of skepticism.

So why did it hurt, when she'd thought herself inured to it long ago? Had she simply gotten unused to thinking about it? Or was it more complicated—was it that it was this man doubting her that made it sting?

She gave herself a mental shake. She'd left all the doubts behind, and she was not going back. She stood up abruptly. "If you don't believe me, then you surely can't believe there's any need for this. Tell Josh so, and we'll both get back to business."

He was on his feet before she could take a step. "I never said I didn't believe you."

"You didn't have to, Mr. Alvera." She saw him wince slightly at the formal appellation, but didn't stop. "I've seen that expression too many times to mistake it."

"What you saw was…shock. Amazement. Astonishment. But not disbelief. You wouldn't lie."

That flat, bald assessment mollified her somewhat. But the way he was looking at her still made her uneasy. She studied him. Tried to separate the tough and efficient agent she knew he was from the darkly handsome, rakish appearance. Tried to think only of his dedication to Josh and to Redstone, and not how the dimple that carved his right cheek when he smiled took him from dangerous to charming in a split second.

"This isn't just going to go away, is it?"

He shook his head. "Nor am I. So we might as well get started."

She was, she thought tiredly, going to have to explain. She sank back into her desk chair, wishing herself anywhere else, confronting any other onerous task.

And when did wishing ever help you out of a bad situation? she asked herself.

"Never," she muttered.

"What?"

She grimaced; she hadn't meant to say it aloud. "Just reminding myself that wishing is for children."

He sat back down himself, and was silent for a moment before he said softly, "Yes, it is. And the day you outgrow wishing is a sad one that comes too early for too many."

Something about his tone enabled her to get it out, what she never talked about. "You want the condensed version?"

"For now," he said, and the implication that there would be more later was nearly as unsettling as his presence.

She braced herself, then began. "Daniel Huntington. Pillar of the community. Wealthy family. Perfect manners. Charming. Polished. Urbane. Blue blood. Only one little glitch in his perfection."

If the staccato presentation registered with him, he didn't show it. His expression never changed when he said, "Which was?"

"He beat his wife."

The emotionless mask vanished for only an instant, but Lilith didn't miss the suddenly feral look that flashed in his eyes.

"The perfect cover," he muttered.

Startled at his quick understanding, she nodded. "Exactly. His stature in the community, his background, his Ivy League upbringing, it all made it nearly impossible for anyone to believe."

Something changed again in his expression. "If it was anyone but you telling me…"

She didn't miss the implication of what he was saying, recognized a second assertion that he'd never not believed her, specifically.

After a moment, he went on. "I didn't think things like that existed in…your world."

A wry sort of amusement quirked one corner of her mouth upward. She perhaps could forgive him more than most; the world he'd grown up in was so radically different, hers must seem like some perfect dream. It spurred her to more explanation than she'd given to anyone in a very long time. "I was as…surprised as you. I never would have believed it if I hadn't lived it. It took me a long time to realize that in Daniel's case, he could only have become what he was in his world."

"But it was your world, too."

"Yes. But I had parents and grandparents who had worked incredibly hard to get where they were. Daniel's family was a few generations down from the workers and felt it was now their place to lead their lessers."

Tony snorted inelegantly, then muttered an apology. She merely smiled. "Exactly how I feel," she said.

A flicker of surprise crossed his face, but all he said was "Go on."

"He was the only son, and was catered to and fawned over from the day he was born. He was raised with a powerful sense of entitlement, that he was born to the elite and deserving of all their privileges. What started as a quick temper and a sense of superiority in the child became a brutal arrogance in the man."

"But he took it out only on you."

She nodded. "He limited it to inside his own home, yes."

"Which makes it worse," Tony said, his voice rough. "It means he had some control. He chose when and where. He chose…"

His voice trailed away, and she finished it for him. "Me. Yes, he did."

"Bastard." He didn't apologize for that one.

"Yes," she agreed calmly.

And she was calm, somewhat to her surprise. Tony Alvera was angry enough for both of them. And that not only surprised her, it warmed her in an odd sort of way. Enough that she was able to go on.

"I found out much later, thanks to Josh and John Draven, that he'd done the same thing to his first wife. But he'd managed to hush it up."

"Did he kill her?" Tony asked, his voice harsh. The possibility obviously didn't startle him.

"No."

"You're sure?"

"Draven is. He found her, talked to her. In her case they paid her off. She took the money and ran. I can't blame her. If I hadn't had Josh standing behind me, I might well have done the same."

He gave her a long, level look. "I don't think so," he said, and something in his gravelly voice touched her. "How did it start with you?"

"It seemed almost accidental. We'd been married six years. I forgave him that time. He'd had a horrible day, a big deal had fallen through, he'd meant to strike the wall, not me, it would never happen again, it was all a mistake…all the usual excuses men like that make." She gave him a wry smile. "He even cried. It was a nice touch."

"Croc tears."

"Yes. But from Daniel Lee Huntington, quite effective. He is—was—perfection personified, the man who had it all, looks, money, position. And I'm the one who destroyed his perfect position in his perfect world."

"He blames you."

It wasn't a question, so she didn't treat it as one. "It was really only thanks to the detective who worked my case," she said. "She devoted herself to taking Daniel down. And she did it, despite pressure from a lot of quarters. The Huntingtons can wield a lot of influence."

"And did?"

She nodded. "To this day, a lot of people in his world support him. Some because they honestly can't believe he would do such a thing, others because they can't afford to cross the Huntingtons."

"What happened? That got him arrested?"

"He had another bad day, nearly a year after the first. He again chose to take it out on me. That was it, for me. I waited until he left, then began to pack. He must have sensed something, because he came back. This time he used a weapon. A fireplace poker."

"Son of a bitch." The curse was whispered, but no less furious. And again Lilith felt that warmth. Silly, she thought. It didn't matter anymore to her who believed her and who didn't. It was the past, long past, behind her and as close to forgotten as it could ever be.

At least, it had been.

"I managed to trip him, and it gave me enough time to get away. I didn't get far before passing out from blood loss." She heard him suck in a breath, but finished it. "Someone found me and called the police."

She stopped there, as if that were the sum total of the story. And for these purposes, it was; the long, horrible nightmare of the trial was not something she wanted to relive in any form.

Tony sat there, looking at her steadily. He didn't prod her for more, or even look as though he had more questions. He looked as if he was seeing what she wasn't saying. And his next words proved her right.

"They put you through hell to put him away, didn't they?"

She saw no point in denying it, especially since that would require exactly what she was trying to avoid, reliving the experience. "They tried. But by then I had help."

"Josh."

"Yes." Then, knowing this was the part Josh would never tell him, she went on. "While I was in the hospital, I saw on the news that Josh was in town. I hadn't seen him in years. I'd spoken to him now and then, but…in any case, I called him. I'm not sure why."

She knew she didn't have to say anything more; no one knew better what it meant to be in trouble and have Josh Redstone on your side.

"You said he's been in for two years."

"Nearly, yes." Guessing what his next question would be, she answered before he had to ask. "His lawyers managed to keep him out for over three, but two years ago his appeals ran out and he was sent to prison. And he was just denied a parole hearing. He thought he should get one sooner than the sentence specified, because…he's special."

Tony smiled at that. It was a smile Lilith thought she wouldn't like to see aimed at her; there was nothing of civil discourse in it, and a great deal of that feral wildness she'd seen flash in his eyes before.

"Good," was all he said.

"So you see why he can't be behind this. I appreciate Josh's concern, but—"

"You can arrange for anything from behind bars. In fact, it's probably easier. A constant flow of people with criminal mindsets, it doesn't take much to find one who's about to get out and willing to do you a favor for a price. Or one who knows somebody who will. And I'm guessing your ex still has the price."

She wondered if he spoke from experience. She knew Josh hadn't pressed charges for his attempted robbery all those years ago, but it didn't seem likely that that had been the first foray into crime for the boy he'd been, the street gangster she'd heard about.

"Oh, yes," she said. "He still has all the assets of the Huntington family. His father died four years ago, and controlling interest in all their varied enterprises passed to Daniel."

"Somebody must be helping him run all that."

"I'm sure the family attorney is dealing. He's very efficient." She grimaced. "As was his criminal attorney. Anyone less than Detective Drake, and the trial might have had a very different outcome."

"Remind me to find her and thank her someday," Tony said, almost under his breath.

Lilith found that curious; it had nothing to do with the current situation, and certainly nothing to do with Tony himself. "Really, I can't believe—"

"If he was out, would you believe he could do this?"

Lilith didn't have to think about that. "Yes."

"And being denied even the possibility of early parole would really set somebody like him off."

Wearily now, she conceded the fact. "Yes. He could never accept that he'd been convicted. Couldn't believe a Huntington would actually be put in prison."

"The pendulum has swung a bit," Tony said.

Lilith's brow furrowed. "How do you mean?"

"The public perception of justice has shifted. Nowadays you're more likely to get hit hard the more prominent you are. Decade or two ago, he'd probably have gotten away with it. Or at least gotten a lesser sentence."

Lilith knew that was likely true. And wondered again just how he'd gained his knowledge of the legal system.

"I'll need to know what his weaknesses are. What will set him off, or oil his jaws."

She blinked. "What?"

"What will get him talking. Or make him mad, if I need to."

For the third time, that fierce, wild look flashed in his eyes. "I'd like that."

"You…you're going to see him?"

"Easiest way to find out if he's behind this. He'll deny it, sure, but if I rattle him enough, he might give himself away."

"He's a very practiced liar," she said.

"So am I, when I need to be," he said negligently.

I'll bet you are, Lilith thought.

The idea didn't please her much.

Chapter 6

Tony tapped a finger restlessly on the steering wheel of his car. As he had been since they'd left Redstone ten minutes ago. "This is a mistake."

"Perhaps."

"You don't need to do this. If you'd just tell me—"

"You said you wanted to rattle him. Make him mad." She gave him a wry grimace of a smile. "I can do that better than anyone."

"How can you want to see him?" Tony asked, barely masking his incredulity.

"Believe me, I don't. I have no desire to ever lay eyes on that man again. But I swore I would never cower from him again, either."

He admired her fortitude, but said, "It's not cowering."

"It is if there's anything to Josh's suspicions, and he's really behind this. If," she added, "there really is a 'this.'"

He didn't tell her that, while he'd been doubtful at first, the moment he'd learned about her ex he'd become as convinced as Josh that there was more to this than just a couple of accidents.

Or perhaps he simply wasn't willing to risk her life on the assumption they'd been mere coincidence.

"I'll handle this," he said firmly. "It's my job, remember?"

"And it's my problem."

He tried another approach. "Would you let me interfere with your work?"

"If it was your area of expertise, yes."

"Exactly." He thought she had just proved his point, but she'd said it too quickly and easily; Lilith Mercer was no fool, and her steely determination was well-known around Redstone.

She proved his unease well-founded with her next words. "And Daniel Huntington is my area of expertise, not yours. If you want to push his buttons, I'm the one who knows what they are."

And just that easily, she had him. And he was going to be stuck in a car with her on the drive that would likely take nearly an hour.

The Redstone name carried a lot of weight in most places, and between Josh himself, John Draven and Josh's mysterious right-hand man, St. John, Tony guessed there weren't many places where one of them didn't know someone. In any case, one phone call had netted them permission to see the prisoner Daniel Huntington as long as they got there within the next two hours. Tony guessed whoever the contact was, he got off duty then.

"You'll need to change," he told her.

She drew back slightly. "What?"

"Your jeans. You can't wear them to visit. Too close to prison blues."

She stared at him, clearly wondering how he knew that, and for some reason he didn't even try to understand he felt compelled to go on, as if in some perverse way he wanted her to be even more aware of the differences between them.

"You can't wear some shades of green, either, because it's too close to the guard uniforms."

"I…see."

"It's my world, Lilith." It hit him then, what he'd been trying to do, to make her keep the distance between them, because he wasn't sure he could. He didn't want to keep doing it, but he couldn't seem to stop. "I know a lot of people in Chino. Gangsters I ran with. Gangsters I ran against. A couple of them are there because they killed my little sister in a drive-by."

She looked at him just long enough to remove her next words from the category of automatic platitude. "I'm sorry."

"Yeah," he muttered, wishing he'd never started this. He hurried her along then, knowing it was going to eat up some of their two-hour window for her to stop and change clothes. But it would give him a chance to look at the scene of this morning's incident, something he wanted to do as soon as possible anyway.

He was surprised when she directed him to a condominium building that looked as if it had once been apartments. It was well kept, and nicely landscaped, but definitely older than the high-rise style buildings that were popping up in the area.

"Twice the space for half the money," she explained, as if she'd read his mind.

So despite her background, she had a practical streak, Tony thought as they started up the stairs to her front door.

"Who cut the wire?" he asked, gesturing to where the ends of the thin silver line were still wrapped around both newel posts of the stairway. He pushed out of his mind the thought of what a miracle it was that she hadn't taken that full tumble, and focused on the evidence left behind.

"I did. My neighbor is seventy-five years old. A fall like that could seriously injure, even kill her."

And a tumble down that flight of concrete stairs could have killed you, he thought.

He crouched to look more closely at the posts as she went inside to change. She was right. A fall like that would have been devastating for her older neighbor.

As if his thoughts had conjured her up, a woman who had to be Mrs. Tilly appeared at the bottom of the stairs, and he realized she must have gotten off the community Dial-A-Ride van that had just pulled out. She had a small bag of groceries and a handful of mail in addition to a capacious black leather purse slung over her right shoulder.

"Is this because of that wire?" the woman asked as she came up the stairs, very spryly for a woman her age, he noted. But she was having trouble with the groceries and the purse slipping off her shoulder, so he instinctively did what he would have done with his mother, who was about the same age; he took the bag. "Let me get that for you."

She looked at him with a touch of wariness he appreciated. "It's all right," he said gently. "I'm not a threat."

"I didn't think you were, or Lilith wouldn't allow you around."

So she knew Lilith well enough to make that assumption. He barely managed to stop himself from probing that knowledge, knowing asking questions would probably have the woman running to Lilith to warn her off.

She let him carry the grocery bag across the landing to her door, where she dug out her keys, opened it, set her purse and the mail inside, then turned back to him and took the bag; she might not be afraid, but she was still cautious. "Are you a policeman or something? Are you here because of what happened?"

"Or something," he said.

"I think it was that little scamp who lives downstairs."

"Lilith told me."

The woman looked thoughtful. "If it wasn't him, who could it have been?"

"I was going to ask you. Did you see anyone around in the morning?"

"Just the gardener," she said. "Although come to think of it, it was a new man, not Jose, who's been here for years."

"You talked to this man?"

"Yes. He said Jose was his cousin, or something like that. And he had all the equipment." She wrinkled her nose. "And tattoos. I don't care for those."

If you only knew, he thought, but managed not to smile. "So he was Hispanic?"

She gave him a wary look, as if she thought he was setting her up to insult him. "Yes," she finally said, and left him standing there on the landing as she went inside.

He was pondering the possible significance of an unknown Hispanic with tattoos when Lilith returned. She'd exchanged those jeans he'd admired for a pair of black twill pants that were almost as distracting, and a crisp, white blouse.

"Here," she said, holding something out to him.

It was a plastic baggie holding a coiled length of silver wire that matched the remnants he'd been looking at.

"Not sure why I saved it. It looks like something you could buy at any hardware store, but there it is."

"Good." He took the bag. "Can't hurt."

He pulled the small, red-handled pocketknife he usually carried out of his left front pocket and made quick work of freeing the two tied ends of the wire. He noticed there were flattened spots on the one end, as if the person tying them had used a tool of some kind, likely pliers, to tighten the wire. He added the ends to the baggie and stuffed it in his jacket pocket. He could have Sam verify whether wire had been sold to any of Lilith's neighbors, at least eliminate that possibility. Sam would love it, tied to a desk as she was….

They headed back down to where his car was parked at the base of the stairs. She didn't go with any more noticeable care than anyone would, clearly not about to let the incident make her afraid of every step. And again he thought of determination.

By the time they were on the freeway headed north, he was realizing the drive wasn't going to be quite the ordeal he'd thought. Whatever her reservations about him had been to begin with, she seemed to either be over them, or at least ignoring them for the moment. She seemed more than willing to just chat amiably.

Or maybe she's just looking for a distraction from having to face her brutal ex, he told himself.

He was still having a bit of trouble absorbing what she'd told him. He realized now how stupid he'd been, thinking that things like that didn't touch her world, but still, it was nearly impossible for him to think of this elegant, classy woman as a victim of such brutality.

And when he did, when he pictured her frightened and in that kind of danger, when he thought of her hurt and bleeding and alone, a rage he hadn't felt since his days on the street welled up in him. The kind of rage that had gotten him into far too much trouble in his life.

Only this time he'd asked for it. Hell, he'd demanded it, demanded to be the one to help her, even knowing it would mean time like this, alone in her company, fighting his tangled feelings every step of the way.

Great.

Masochist didn't even begin to describe it.

"I think," Lilith said when the conversation turned, as it inevitably did between people who had their particular boss in common, "you have to have the most amazing 'How I met Josh' story in all of Redstone."

"The most infamous, maybe," he said as he signaled for a lane change to get out from behind a truck spitting rocks off its uncovered load. They were in the Redstone car he drove on assignment, but he took care of it as if it were his own, she noticed.

"That, too," she agreed with a laugh, and was oddly gratified when that made him smile, perhaps because it looked as if it was in spite of himself.

"I owe Josh my life," he said simply. "And not just for not having my…butt thrown in jail back then."

She didn't miss the change of words, and wondered if it was because she was female, or older than he, or simply that she was Redstone and therefore deserved the respect Josh demanded for all his people.

"I heard he sent you to school."

Tony nodded, although he didn't look at her. It wasn't because there was a lot of traffic at this midday hour, but maybe he was just a careful driver, she thought.

"Yes." She saw one corner of his mouth quirk. "It was his price for staying out of juvie. I'd been there twice, and I didn't want to go back."

This, she hadn't known. Either part. "His price?"

"He told me I could go to this school he knew about, or I could go back in the system. My choice."

She laughed; she couldn't help it. "That's Josh. Giving you options but making the right one all but impossible to pass up."

He did glance at her then. "Well, I wasn't sure it was the right one. To me, then, school was just another form of jail."

"I'm sorry to hear that."

"I'll bet you loved school. Becoming a teacher and all."

"I did love school," she said. "At least, until I got old enough to realize that I was being fed somebody's particular version of the world, to be memorized and spewed back when required."

"Sounds like school to me," he said dryly.

"I wanted the truth," she said, "and to learn how to learn for myself. And that's why I thought I wanted to be a teacher. To teach that. But when the trouble with my husband began, he used his influence to have me laid off. He didn't want me working."

"Hurt his self-image?"

"No, teaching was acceptable. It was control. He couldn't keep me sufficiently under his thumb if I was out working every day."

A little bitterness had crept into her voice, and it startled her. She'd thought herself long past such a feeling. Determined to end this now, she turned the conversation back to him. "So Josh made you go back to school?"

He accepted the change with surprising ease; perhaps he had sensed her discomfort. "Not back. To a different school. A college prep academy. I thought he was crazy. Me, in some snobby, upper-crust college prep? I laughed in his face."

Since she had gone to such a place herself, Lilith had a full album of images to draw on. She couldn't picture the kid he'd been in any of them. Nor could she begin to imagine how hard it must have been for him.

"But he didn't give up," she said.

"No. I told him it was a joke, no place like that would ever let somebody like me in. He said that was his problem."

"And they did."

"Turns out it was run by a friend of his."

"He has them everywhere, doesn't he?"

"That's because he helps people everywhere."

"I've often thought," Lilith said, "that if Josh ever called in all the favors he's owed at once, he could run the world."

"And it'd be a better place," Tony said.

"That it would," she agreed. "So, after that college prep, what happened?"

"College." He said it lightly, a small joke. But she was looking at him, saw the expression that flitted across his face, and guessed he'd still not quite gotten over the unexpectedness of it. "Business major. Which," he said, still lightly, "as you can see, I'm not really using."

She could not for the life of her imagine him tied to a desk. "Where?"

"U.C.L.A."

She blinked; she hadn't known that. "Great school."

"Yes." He flicked a glance at her. "And I've paid Josh back. Every cent of the tuition he put into me."

Somehow that didn't surprise her, although she knew Josh

would never have expected it. She wondered for a moment what it had taken for him to get Josh to accept the payback. That, she decided, must have been quite a discussion.

As if he'd read her thoughts, she saw him smile. "He fought me when I started, so I put it all into an account I never touched. Then I handed it over. He finally took it, but only for the next person he decided to help. It became the Redstone Scholarship Fund."

She smiled in turn. "That is so Josh it doesn't even require a comment."

That it was Tony as well didn't escape her.

She studied him for a moment. His hands were relaxed on the steering wheel and one elbow was resting casually on the armrest of the driver's seat. Logic, and her knowledge that Redstone Security was known worldwide even in traditional law enforcement circles, told her he might be relaxed now, but if anything happened, he would turn into what he was, a trained agent. John Draven would have seen to that.

But there was something more in this man, something somehow more intense than even Draven, who had arrived at Redstone via the military, a veteran of battles in various parts of the world, including the one that had taken from Josh his brother and last surviving relative.

Tony Alvera had been in only one war, but it was an insidious one that claimed casualties in a way that seemed little different to her.

Except that it took place at home, where kids should have been safe.

It struck her then that it was no small miracle that this man was here, now, where he was. And while he might want to give all the credit to Josh, she knew better. It didn't take much imagination to figure out he'd had to fight every step of the way.

She suspected the thing he'd had to fight hardest was himself.

Chapter 7

She had acted, Tony thought as they waited in the visiting area, as if they were simply going for a pleasant drive. Totally at ease, as if he were a casual acquaintance she didn't mind spending time with.

Why not, since that's all you are? he told himself.

Of course, she wasn't feeling any of the internal tension he was feeling. She had no idea that he'd volunteered for—or to be honest, commandeered—this assignment, let alone why. So why should she feel anything but relaxed?

And if she did know?

His first thought was that she'd run, screaming. But his second thought was no, she wouldn't, she had too much class for that. She'd think of some graceful, tactful way to deflect his idiocy, and probably try to do it without being cruel.

But she wasn't happy to be here, that he could see. She kept looking around, the only sign of nerves he'd seen in her, which was a testament to her determination.

"Depressing," she muttered.

"Yes," Tony agreed.

"'In case of lockdown,'" she read off a posted sign on one wall that explained what visitors must do.

"Doesn't happen often, not during visiting hours. They're pretty much sacrosanct."

"I'm sure no one wants to lose a chance to see the people they care about."

"Not to mention that that's when they get their contraband," he said dryly. "Nobody wants to risk that."

She went still, then turned away from the posted sign to look at him steadily. "What is it you're after, Mr. Alvera? Am I supposed to assume you know all these things because you're Redstone Security, or because you're a badass yourself?"

He couldn't believe elegant Lilith Mercer had said that. Her casual use of the term startled him into gaping at her. As did her perceptiveness, realizing he'd done it on purpose.

He had no answer to her second question, at least none he wanted to share with her, so he took refuge in the first.

"It would be nice if you'd quit calling me 'Mr. Alvera.' We were at least on a first name basis before."

"You weren't digging into *my* life before," she said wryly, but she gave in gracefully and smiled at him as she added, "Tony."

That smile did crazy things to him, and he welcomed the arrival of a uniformed corrections officer to escort them to the visiting area.

While he'd asked for a private room, he'd made clear that in no way was this to be a contact visit. He didn't want Daniel Huntington anywhere within reach of the woman he'd once tried to murder, even with guards close at hand. There was a table, with chairs on both sides, and Tony guessed this room was usually used by lawyers visiting clients. Lilith stared at the setup, and he wondered if she was thinking of the kinds of people who had sat in these plastic chairs over the years. If she was wondering how on earth she'd ended up in a place like this, even for a moment.

He couldn't think of a place more contrary to who and what she was. And he couldn't imagine how she must feel, being here, for this reason.

Startling him, she reached for the back of one of the chairs, pulled it out from the table and sat down, crossing her legs at the knees and leaning back casually as if she were sitting in a friend's living room. As if this didn't bother her at all.

Tony realized she'd been contemplating what scenario she wanted her ex-husband to see when he came in: a nervous, frightened ex-wife who was still his victim, or a calm, cool woman who wasn't afraid of him at all.

Bravo, Lilith, he thought, wishing he had the nerve to say it out loud. He stayed on his feet; if he had to take Huntington down—an action he would savor to the max—he didn't want to waste time kicking a chair out of his way.

The sound of a door opening drew his attention, and he snapped to full alert. His first impression of the man they'd come to see was jumbled. As Daniel Huntington walked through the door, a guard close behind him, Tony wondered what the hell it was that let guys like him look sophisticated even in jail garb. Even now, he oozed upper crust in a way Tony knew, for all his acquired polish, he himself could only fake. There was just something in the way Huntington walked, the way he carried himself. Even his smooth, superior expression made his surroundings seem irrelevant. He didn't look as if this place had touched him at all, and Tony guessed he'd been able to buy his personal safety as easily as he'd bought his way out of charges from his first wife.

Even now, the man looked as if he'd walked off the cover of *GQ* or something, Tony thought. No wonder nobody had believed that he could do something as classless and crude as beat up women. It all fit—that perfect, chiseled face, the blond hair and icy blue eyes, the haughty air….

But not the fear that flashed in those eyes. It was there for only a split second—if he hadn't been studying the man so carefully he would have missed it, but he was certain it had been there. Certain in the way he'd once been able to judge whether guys on the street would run or fight.

This was the kind of guy who'd order a drive-by, but never do the dirty work himself. Not if there was a possibility the victim might be able to fight back.

The smirk that accompanied Daniel Huntington's first words made Tony want to smack him down right now.

"Hello, my sweet wife. Finally missed me too much to stay away?"

Tony didn't know if Lilith was going to answer—she was staring at the man as if he'd crawled out from some dark, dank place—but he spoke before she had the chance.

"Ground rules," he said, letting every bit of the animus he was feeling show in his voice. And in his face, since his back was to Lilith at the moment. "You sit. You stay on your side of the table. You keep your hands on that table. You don't so much as lean forward. If I don't like the way you breathe, I'll put you on the floor. Got it?"

Huntington looked him up and down. He was cool now, that moment of fear vanquished and likely forgotten; this was the man who'd nearly fooled a jury into believing Lilith was a disturbed woman who'd made all this up.

"Bought yourself a pit bull, have you?" he sneered, glancing at Lilith.

Lilith simply looked back at him, much as if he were some sort of ugly anomaly whose existence she was pondering.

"Charming, as always," Lilith said, and Tony marveled at the amusement in her voice. If she was faking it, she was doing a masterful job; Huntington's jaw tightened slightly.

"Fitting. Does he service you like the bitch that you are?"

Tony's hands wanted to curl into fists.

Lilith's smile only widened. "Poor, inadequate Danny. He's much, much better at it than you ever were."

It took all Tony had to keep his expression even and his mouth shut. He knew she was doing exactly what she was here for—pushing Huntington's buttons—but he wished she'd chosen a different one first.

He focused grimly on his job, ignoring the images her words had started cascading through his mind. She'd obviously been right about knowing their quarry, because for an instant sheer fury showed in Huntington's face. Tony guessed it stemmed from the insecurity that was at the base of many abusers, and from the possessiveness of a man like Huntington, who couldn't abide the thought of anything he'd once owned belonging to someone else.

"It's nice to know I can still get to you," Lilith said, as if she were discussing the weather.

"You never could," Huntington declared.

"Dear boy," Lilith said, in a tone Tony had always associated with society mavens, "then why are you so angry?"

"Bitch," he said.

"I must say, your vocabulary has degenerated since you've been here with all your fellow convicts."

Huntington started out of his chair. Tony sensed the action the moment before the man made it, and with a darting move he slammed his forearm across Huntington's upper chest, slapping the man back into the chair, nearly knocking it and him over like a beetle tossed helplessly on its back.

The guard coughed but never moved. Tony thought it was a quiet warning until he flicked the uniformed man a glance and saw approval in his expression. Then the man looked away, pretending he'd seen nothing. Tony straightened, towering over the seated man now.

Huntington looked startled and off guard, so Tony struck fast, spitting out the question with all the fury he himself was feeling.

"Who did you hire?"

"I don't know what you're talking about."

"You know damned well what I'm talking about. Was the plan murder, since you failed when you tried?"

Tony couldn't be sure if the man's sudden tautness was because he'd struck home with the truth, or merely at the accusation of failure; he was fairly certain the latter would get to the likes of Huntington more.

He pressed, leaning in until Huntington reacted, and wariness came into those icy blue eyes.

"You sent somebody after her, and I want to know who it was."

"After her? Why on earth would I do that? She's nothing. Less than nothing."

Then why the insults? Tony told him silently. That was not the reaction of a man to a woman who meant nothing to him. Even hatred was a form of saying someone mattered to you.

"I know you set it up. And I will find out how and who you sent. When I do, your life here is going to be even more miserable."

"I did nothing," Huntington declared. "Why don't you ask her who else she's made angry enough to want to give her what she deserves."

"Was it somebody who was getting out? Cell mate?"

Huntington glared at him. Tony leaned in.

"Maybe just *your* mate? Whose bitch are you?" Tony used the word purposefully, turning it back on the man who had thrown it at Lilith. He knew the moment he'd said it, however, that he'd blown it. He'd let his emotions override his cool.

"Go to hell," Huntington said. His face went tight and stubborn, and Tony knew he had shut down. He refused to say another word, and at last Tony had to signal the guard that they were through.

"That went well," Tony muttered under his breath as they cleared security and started out of the building. He gave her a sideways glance, but was unable to read anything in her expression. "I'm sorry. I blew it in there."

"It was worth it."

He stopped in his tracks. She halted a couple of steps later, and turned to look at him.

"I just made this whole thing harder," Tony pointed out. "He'll never talk now. So how is that worth it?"

"It was worth it to me," she amended. "Because I wasn't afraid of him."

Tony's expression softened. One corner of his mouth lifted in a crooked smile. "No, you weren't. You were iced. It was him who was nothing to you."

"Yes."

"Okay, it was worth it, then."

His abrupt about-face seemed to amuse her, and she smiled back at him.

He was contemplating the effects of that smile, a little amazed that she wasn't angry with him for having made a hash out of the interview. He'd always known, simply because of the kind of person who was Redstone, that there was much more to her than the polished, refined exterior. That had been proven to him during Logan Beck's case, when she had gone out of her way to allow Liana to help the ex-cop. She'd barely known her new assistant, hadn't known Beck at all, but she'd gone to the wall for them both, right along with Josh.

By the time they were outside in the spring sunshine he was feeling a little better, and he didn't think it was entirely due to getting out of the oppressive surroundings. They got to the car and he opened the door for her. She thanked him with another smile, obviously having no problem with having a door opened for her, and as he went around to the driver's side he was feeling much better.

He pulled the driver's door open, turned to get in. And the view he got of the California Institute for Men jolted him back to reality.

If not for the grace of Josh Redstone, there was a grimly real chance he would have wound up there, or someplace like it. Or worse, like Chaco Ramirez, who'd ended up in Pelican Bay, locked down twenty-three hours a day.

Instead, he'd been in school—although he wasn't sure the battle for acceptance there was much easier than the battle to stay alive and well in prison. And then college, and then further training under the wing of Redstone, in anything that had interested him. And some that didn't; his street brothers would have laughed as he learned about table manners and the right fork, but Josh had insisted.

He'd come a long way, true.

But no matter how far he'd come, he still hadn't reached the point where Lilith Mercer—or Daniel Huntington—had started.

He never would.

Chapter 8

Lilith sat in the Redstone car in silence, marveling a little over what had just happened. She felt a quiet, inner satisfaction that she had experienced only the tiniest of inner lurches when Daniel had walked into that room.

She knew nothing had shown on the outside, but that had never been a requirement; Daniel could always sense her fear. It told him how far he could go—when he knew someone was afraid of him, any boundaries fell away. But today, there had been nothing.

She had been, as Tony had so aptly put it, iced.

But to her surprise, the greater satisfaction came from something else, something that surprised her. She had never thought of herself as vengeful, but she couldn't deny that she had taken a certain pleasure in seeing suave, sophisticated Daniel Huntington treated like the dog he'd called Tony.

And even more pleasure that her "pit bull" had turned on him. The words played back in her mind, and she looked away, out the passenger window, not certain she could hide her odd reaction.

Does he service you like the bitch that you are?

Daniel had said it, of course, to insult her. It was crude, and coarse, and meant to convince her she wasn't good enough for his world.

Funny how, instead, the abusive words had sent thoughts and images roaring through her brain that now made her afraid to turn her face to the man Daniel had been speaking about.

He's much, much better at it than you ever were.

Her answer had been calculated to enrage him. And it had.

But it had also intensified those vivid images racing through her mind, until she had felt her heart begin to pound in her chest as her pulse picked up.

Because she had little doubt that the slap aimed at her ex-husband was true. Little doubt because, she told herself, Daniel had been a perfunctory lover when calm, and a painfully rough one when angry.

It had nothing to do with what kind of lover Tony Alvera was. That was something she'd never know.

She told herself that, given how many women probably already knew, that was a very good thing. And then she told herself again.

She steadied herself, forced herself to look at the man in the driver's seat, wondering why they were still sitting in the prison parking area, why he hadn't even turned the key.

Unusually for her, she felt the strain of silence and finally spoke. "So now you know."

"Now I know what?"

"How shockingly bad my judgment can be."

"Was, maybe back then."

She appreciated the assumption that it had improved.

"But that mask he wears is pretty good."

"I was hoping never to see it again. I had relegated all that to the past."

"The past," he said quietly, "is part of what made us who we are today. You may not think about it, but it's always there."

It wasn't a stretch to realize he wasn't just talking about her. And for all the painful experience she'd gone through with Daniel, it had been only a few years. She'd been an adult, and she'd enjoyed a fairly happy and secure childhood. For Tony Alvera, there had been none of that respite; he'd had to start fighting as a child, probably younger than she cared to think about.

"Did he always talk to you like that?" he asked.

She was almost grateful for the disruption of her thoughts. The tangle of imagining what this man had been through—and her own out-of-hand imaginings about him—were getting stickier by the minute.

"No. If he had, I would never have married him, no matter who he was or how happy it made my parents. It was only later on that that kind of thing started. I've often tried to figure out if there was something, some incident that set him off, because for the first six years of our marriage, he was…normal."

"But you never found anything?"

"No. Nothing that stood out to me, anyway. On the surface at least, things were…if not happy, at least pleasant. Then the insults started. My family, according to him, were latecomers to wealth, whereas his had been old money. Generations of old money."

"Built on what?" Tony asked, surprising her with how quickly he asked the key question.

"Smuggling," she said, confirming his guess. "Back in the day it gave them enough to buy their way into academia, politics, and they used the mask of public service to hide their origins. It worked. Now people either don't know—an ignorance I have to confess to—or choose to forget where the Huntingtons made their fortune."

"So now they're legit."

"Oh, I'm sure their fingers are in a few things that would raise eyebrows. The polish is only a veneer. A very thick one after all these years, but underneath, they're the same cutthroats that used to lure ships onto the rocks so they could steal the cargo, and the drowning crew be damned."

"Nice."

"And Daniel is the culmination of all those years of polish and wealth."

"And he tried to murder you. How can you be so calm about it? About him?"

She smiled at that. "I wasn't, not always. It took a long time to reach the assurance that one man was not all men, and my ex-husband was not worth becoming a frightened, timid person for."

Something shifted in his steady gaze then. His expression changed. It took her a moment to realize that what she was seeing was undisguised admiration.

An odd sort of warmth flooded her. She tried to gather her thoughts, to control this strange, unknown response to a simple look.

Except there was nothing simple about the look Tony Alvera had turned on her. And she was finally forced to admit that part of the satisfaction she'd felt had been because he'd lost his cool, on her behalf. He'd jumped Daniel in her defense. Somehow the fact that he'd lost his cool because Daniel had insulted her made it much more personal.

But personal was exactly what this couldn't become, she told herself. Still, she wanted to say something to him. She tried to put into words something she'd been thinking since the moment her ex-husband had walked into that visiting room.

"Daniel was born to a world of privilege, and that's the facade he presents to the world, but underneath it all, he's the worst kind of slime."

"That," Tony said, "goes without saying. I've seen street killers with more class. At least they don't hide what they are."

"And that's the world you were born to," she said, thoughtfully. "But you worked your way out."

"Josh gave me that—" he began, but stopped when she shook her head.

"You know as well as I do Josh doesn't believe in handouts. He may have given you the opportunity, the hand up, but you did it yourself. You worked, fought and probably clawed your way out. Now, *that's* something to be admired."

For a long moment he simply stared at her, looking stunned. She'd known his story—at least, the versions that circulated at Redstone—but never really thought of it beyond the surface. Now, after having been inside that prison and seeing where he could so easily have ended up, she felt an even greater sense of amazement.

In an odd, unexpected sort of way, she felt proud of him.

That's it, she told herself. You're proud of him. Proud of him like…like a doting aunt would be.

Because she was old enough to be his aunt, she knew. She wasn't sure exactly how much older she was, but enough.

At least you're not old enough to be his mother, she muttered inwardly.

She refused to think about why that small fact made her thankful.

"I blew it," Tony said at the end of his report, his voice grim as he faced his boss. He'd dropped Lilith off at Redstone Headquarters and come straight back to report.

John Draven looked at him in that cool, calculating way that made anybody with sense realize he was messing with somebody who could take him down in an instant. And would, if he thought he had to.

After a moment, Draven simply said, "Why?"

Tony blinked. "What?"

"Why did you blow it?"

Leave it to Draven to cut to the crux of things. "I just did," Tony muttered.

"You're one of the coolest agents we've got. You *never* lose your composure. Even when Lisa was killed, you stayed cool and finished the job."

Tony winced inwardly, as he always did at the mention of Lisa. She'd been the first woman he'd ever thought about forever with. And he'd gotten forever, all right. The only forever anyone was ever guaranteed—forever dead.

"Always a first time," he muttered. He shifted uncomfortably, as much because of Draven's scrutiny as from having to admit to his mistake.

"So why now?"

The only answer Tony had was something Draven wasn't going to want to hear, something that would likely get him pulled off the case.

"Is this something to do with why you lobbied for this assignment in the first place?"

He should have known Draven would make the connection. Knowing he had no real choice, he answered. Carefully. "I told you. I worked with her on Beck's case. We got along. I thought she might prefer somebody she knew, at least a little, rather than a stranger poking around in her business."

He was sure his demand to be assigned to this had been far more strident than that casual explanation made it seem, just as he was sure that fact was obvious to his boss. But he wasn't ready to go any further. In part because he didn't really have an answer to Draven's question.

Why now? Why lose it now, when he'd been fine working with her during the entire thing with Beck and Liana? Was it simply because then the focus had been on them, and not on Lilith? He'd felt the same way then, and working with her had only expanded his admiration. She was tireless, and more than once Liana had remarked that Lilith could wear *her* out. He could see that himself now; she never seemed to slow down.

Or was it something stupider? Had working with her, talking

with her, seeing her concern for Liana and her cop even though she barely knew either of them, weakened the barriers he'd built? Had he somehow lowered his guard, let impossible ideas into his head?

He jammed those thoughts back into that cage in his mind that seemed to be getting fuller and harder to close these days. And when he spoke again—as he had to, in response to Draven's silent, patient waiting—it was again the truth.

"Lilith is a classy, kind, generous lady. He talked to her like she was some twenty-dollar streetwalker. It pissed me off."

"I see." For an instant Tony thought Draven was fighting a smile, but that seemed so impossible he knew he had to be wrong. "I suppose I should be glad you left him alive, then."

"It was close," Tony muttered.

"Your tux clean?"

Tony nearly gaped at his boss, nonplussed by the abrupt non sequitur. "What?"

"Your tux," Draven repeated with an exaggerated air of patience.

Tony gambled on yes, because he always had it cleaned after the rare occasion when he was required to wear the thing. He wouldn't have one at all if Josh hadn't insisted there would be occasions when he would need it. "Uh…yes."

"Good. Because you'll be taking your…assignment to Josh's Back to Life prosthetics fund-raiser tonight. Under wraps, of course, so you'll have to act like an escort, not a bodyguard."

Automatically, Tony cataloged the reason for the event. Redstone R&D had been the leader in that field of research ever since Ian Gamble came up with the prosthetic foot that had revolutionized the entire endeavor.

Then the rest hit him.

Tux. Escort. Fund-raiser.

They all added up to formal. He groaned inwardly. It wasn't

that he couldn't dress up—he had, on several occasions, when the assignment demanded it.

He'd just never done it as somebody's escort before.

Lilith's escort.

He fought down the rising tide of heat that was building within him. God, what if she wore that red dress again? What if he had to look at her like that, sticking close to her side like a good bodyguard, all evening?

He opened his mouth to suggest someone else do it. He just wasn't sure who. Rand Singleton would be perfect—he could picture Rand, who was even blonder and almost as beautiful, with Lilith—but he and his wife, Kate, were still ensconced in the woods west of Seattle, keeping Redstone Northwest safe and running smoothly.

"This is a direct request from Josh, so if there's a problem, Alvera, tell me now. I'll put Taylor on the case and you can go get your head together, or whatever you need to do."

"No," he said instantly. The last thing he wanted was a brand-new headquarters agent, no matter what her outside experience, responsible for Lilith's safety. He would simply have to get his head back in the game, and fast.

"I know you hate these things," Draven said. "I'm not fond of them myself. But it's only a few hours. You can stand anything for a few hours."

I'd rather be tortured, Tony thought, but wisely kept that thought to himself; somehow he didn't think it would be well received by a man who wouldn't take it as a figure of speech. Draven had personal experience with torture, and the scars to prove it.

Still, Tony thought as he left the airport office of Redstone Security, there was physical pain, and then there was nonphysical. And sometimes the nonphysical kind was worse.

Problem was, he was very much afraid this could turn into both.

Chapter 9

"Josh, really, it's a public event, with a lot of people. I hardly need a bodyguard under the circumstances."

"Sorry, Lil. Not negotiable."

Josh's voice held that note she knew so well, implacable, immovable. The voice that so startled unsuspecting folk who took his regular speech at face value and assumed he was as slow as his lazy drawl. If he were here instead of on the phone, she knew exactly what expression he'd be wearing, only his eyes giving away the steely resolve.

"Don't worry," he said then, a glimmer of humor changing his tone, "he cleans up pretty nice. Better than I do."

Lilith chuckled at that; Josh hated putting his tall, lanky body into formal wear, and his usual lament was that he was much happier in jeans and cowboy boots. Even Lilith, who'd never been closer to a cowboy than a movie or TV screen, had to admit that the attire suited him, made her see the almost universal appeal.

It wasn't until they'd hung up that the other part of what he'd said really registered.

Don't worry, he cleans up pretty nice.

"Oh, I'm sure he does," she murmured under her breath.

He was amazing enough already. With that easy, practiced charm he seemed to turn on so effortlessly, he reminded her a little too much of Daniel. But unlike Daniel, where the veneer was all there was, where the charm dripped from every pore only in public, in Tony it was a striking counterpoint to his edgy, dangerous looks. Even if you didn't know his background, anyone could sense the edge was sharp and the danger real.

There was, she knew, a type of woman who was drawn to that particular paradox. She'd never thought herself one of them.

And you aren't drawn to Tony Alvera, of all people, she told herself firmly.

She even believed it. It had simply been a very long time since she'd had a man around with any regularity, and having this one practically in her pocket all the time was unsettling. That was all.

The problem was hers, she knew. He was simply doing his job, and doing it with the thoroughness and determination that was the Redstone hallmark. If he had the slightest clue she was even having these thoughts, he'd likely laugh in her face.

No, he wouldn't do that. That would be Daniel. Tony would never laugh at someone in the family. He was probably used to such things, given the number of those women she'd been speculating about.

However, he would also likely ask to be pulled from this assignment, and rightfully so.

And that would solve my problem, wouldn't it?

It would. But the image of how that request would sound, of Tony going to Draven, or worse, Josh, and explaining why he couldn't stay on this assignment, was so hideously humiliating that she couldn't even think it through.

Since asking Josh to call the whole thing off had been fruitless so far, she had no choice but to deal.

And deal she would. She'd stood up to Daniel Huntington, so this should be nothing. She simply had to make certain that the man Josh had glued to her never got the slightest clue that the woman who was merely a job to him was having thoughts that would mortify them both. If she was ten years younger…

But she wasn't. And that alone was enough for her to quash those thoughts and get on with her day. At least here, in Redstone Headquarters, she was allowed to be alone and focus on her work.

So focus, she ordered herself silently.

Still, it took her a while before she could completely free her mind of Tony's presence. But after she caught herself wondering what he was doing right now, she summoned up the will to shut that part of her mind off. She had a job to do, too, and she was as dedicated to doing it as her charming shadow was.

She called up the computer file she'd been reading when the phone had rung and went back to searching for hints of any more damage to the place that had become as much her home and family as her blood one.

The raucous catcalls and whistles followed him down the grim, graffiti-laden street. He plastered a cocky grin on his face, held up his arms to show off the expensive leather coat he'd purposefully chosen for this expedition, and spun slowly as he walked, giving a slight bow when he was done.

The grins and shouts he got in response told him the show had been effective; they were treating him like one of their own made good. He knew they were likely assuming he'd made good in ways the cops would like to know about, probably thinking he was dealing in drugs or women, and that could only help his cause.

It felt strange to be here. It wasn't that he hadn't been back before; he had. He'd been careful to see that no one here knew the real reason behind his disappearance all those years ago. For all they knew, he'd been in prison somewhere else, and he let them keep thinking it. There had been no one left behind to tell the truth, anyway; his little sister was long dead, and thanks to Josh he'd moved his parents out of this hell within weeks after his foolish yet fortunate attempt to mug the young then-millionaire.

Before, when he'd come back, he'd simply thought how lucky he was to be out. This time, his feelings were more tangled, and he wasn't sure why.

He kept going. This had been his neighborhood, once. And more than once he'd used that, because people on the street had a way of knowing things you'd never expect them to know. Including whether there was anyone recently out of jail or prison who had come out with a job to do. True, the possibility was tenuous—a new gardener who happened to be Hispanic wasn't much of a connection—but thanks to his misstep with Huntington, it was all he had.

He hadn't really planned on doing this today. He'd thought he would keep digging into Lilith's ex's past, see what he could find. As far as Tony was concerned, the man was still the prime suspect, although he was honest enough to realize he'd like nothing better than to add time to the charming, urbane, sophisticated and rotten-inside Daniel Huntington's sentence.

But after Draven had informed him what he'd be doing this evening, he'd changed his plans. And about then his self-honesty had fallen short; on some level he knew he'd come there intentionally, to pound home the differences between them by revisiting his past in a literal sense, but he wasn't admitting that up front.

Not yet, anyway.

But here he was, after dressing with care in the kind of clothes that he knew would scream *success* to the people he'd be encountering. And as he'd put on the clothes he'd also put on the attitude, the arrogant swagger he'd grown up emulating, wanting to have for real, because it was the only way out that he could see.

And he'd wanted out. Long before the day his little sister had died from a stray bullet fired by a drive-by shooter, and he'd seen his mother become a faint shadow of her former, vibrant self and his father, always a reserved man, shut down completely, he'd wanted out. Wanted *them* out.

He hadn't missed the irony that the only way out seemed to be using the very things that made him want to get out. Getting out took money, and the gangs and their hierarchy seemed the only option; if he rose high enough, and his cut of their illegal activities got big enough, then he could afford it.

Of course, if you got that high, you could never leave. They'd kill you first.

But he could get his parents out. And then, if he had to leave everything, including his family, to get out himself, he would.

He shook himself out of the swamp of memories; not paying attention on these streets could get you killed. He kept walking, noticing there weren't any familiar faces among those he passed. Some eyed him with suspicion, some with disgust, some with envy. The flashy coat, he thought wryly, was working. It was warm enough on this late spring day to make it clear he was wearing it either to show off or to hide something beneath it—a weapon, he was sure, most of them thought—and either reason contributed to the effect he wanted.

As he kept going, he wondered if the East Side 13s had all been killed off and he'd somehow missed it. Then he laughed inwardly at himself; the ones he'd run with were his age now, and a whole new batch had likely taken over, probably guys who were just toddlers when he'd been here.

Once he saw a woman he thought he recognized, but she darted away from him too quickly to be sure. He kept going, certain that whatever else had changed, the grapevine on the streets hadn't, and that whoever was running the ES 13s these days would know about this intruder sooner rather than later.

He was proven right about three blocks from the heart of their turf.

"*¡Orale, vato!*"

The "Hey, dude," hail from behind turned him on his heel. He was a little startled to finally see a familiar face. "*Rico. ¿Que pasa?*"

More than the casual what's-up inquiry, he wondered what Rico Morales was doing here. And even more than that, he wondered when his onetime friend had gotten out of jail.

"*¿Tienes un cigarro, mijo?*"

"Sorry," Tony said to the request, switching to English, "I quit smoking."

"You quit a lot of things, bro." Rico made the switch as easily as he did.

"Some," Tony said, "I never started." Thanks to Josh, I never had to.

Rico, however, had never shown any interest in getting out. His greatest aspiration had been to be a loyal ESer. And he'd gone to jail to prove it, taking the fall for the leader of the gang in a drive-by case like the one that had killed Lucinda.

But Rico had also had a bit of a teenage crush on Lucy, and therefore had never given Tony much heat on those rare occasions when he went back to the neighborhood.

"When did you get out?" he asked.

Rico frowned at him. "I been out six months, *vato*. You ever come around anymore, you'd know that."

"Been busy."

Rico eyed the leather coat. "Yeah, you have."

The man didn't ask at what, for which Tony was thankful. What he'd done since he left the streets wasn't known here, and he wanted to keep it that way. Let them think what they thought, that he'd made it dealing drugs or pimping whores, as long as the conduit for information didn't dry up. It was the one thing he had to offer Redstone that no one else had, and he knew it.

Someday he would come back here and show others there was another way, passing along what Josh had done for him in his own small way, but right now he was leaving well enough alone. "Anybody else local get out lately? Like in the last month or so?"

Rico lifted a brow at him. "Why you want to know?"

"Looking for someone."

"Who?"

"Don't have a name. Just heard he took on a job for a friend of mine, in Chino. Might have something else worth his while to do."

Rico eyed the coat again. "Hey, I can do whatever you need doing, my old friend."

"You find me this guy," Tony said with a grin, "and you can have this coat."

Rico laughed, but the sound faded when he realized Tony was serious. "What else do you know about this guy you are looking for?"

"Job was getting rid of my friend's ex-wife."

Rico laughed. "She cheat on him while he was inside?"

"No."

His answer was quick and certain. Too quick, he realized instantly; it would have been the easiest explanation. But it had been instinctive; Lilith would never cheat. That would be more Huntington's style.

"Before." He knew he'd have to get more specific, make something up that sounded real enough, and it made him edgy. "She's some wheel at that big-time place, Redstone, Incorporated. It was somebody there. That's why he's inside."

"He had to teach her a lesson," Rico said with a nod, accepting the story with complete understanding. In his world, it made perfect sense.

"Know anybody who took on a job like that, when they got out? Or anybody who knows anybody?"

"I could ask," Rico said. "I have a lot of friends."

Tony got the subtext, that after doing his time Rico had moved up in the ranks and could call on other gang members to do this for him.

"I know you do. Why I came to you," he said, paying the requisite respect. "Anything you find, anything about a job like that, or anything connected to that Redstone place, would be worth a lot to me."

"I would need to thank them for their help," Rico said pointedly.

"I'll make sure the pockets in the coat aren't empty," Tony promised.

Rico seemed to consider this for a moment, obviously wondering if he could trust this man who'd left them in the dust years ago. Finally, Rico nodded. "I will ask."

Tony reached into his pocket and took out a business card. It was blank except for a single phone number. He'd had them made for just such occasions. "My pager. Use it if you turn anything up. If it's the right thing, the right person, I'll make sure there's more than the coat in it for you."

Rico took the card, looked at it, then looked at Tony speculatively. "What is it that pays so well, *mijo?*"

"Pal," Tony echoed in English, "you wouldn't believe me if I told you."

Chapter 10

"Stop it!"

Lilith snapped the order to her image in the mirror as she fussed with her hair yet again. So far she'd had it down in a sleek fall, then curled into waves, then up, then down again.

She was acting, she thought with rueful self-awareness, as if this was a date. A first date. With someone she wanted to impress.

Disgusted with herself, she finally pulled her hair into a classic French twist, secured it quickly with the ease of long practice, tugged a few strands loose to soften the look and let it go at that.

And she was *not,* she told herself firmly, going to second-guess what she was going to wear tonight. She had a limited choice for formal occasions, having long ago gotten rid of the expansive wardrobe of gowns and shoes and bags she'd required as the wife of Daniel Huntington. She'd donated them to a charity the week she'd gotten out of the hospital, wanting nothing from that time in her life, no reminders except one—she kept the photographs the police had taken of her injuries.

At first, she'd kept them to remind herself of her near-fatal lapse in judgment. Later, she kept them to use when she spoke to groups at women's shelters. She knew the image she presented, knew it resulted in the kind of disbelief she so often encountered, that such things could ever happen in the world she had lived in. But one look at those photos, and the women she talked to knew that what she told them was true; she had indeed walked in their shoes. And then they listened to her, knowing she understood.

She brushed off the old memories, hating that they'd been stirred up again when she'd thought them safely and securely buried. She forced herself to focus on the task at hand, getting out the floor-length gown she'd chosen. It was one of two she owned in her favorite red. The other was more daring, lower cut and clingy enough to warrant some care about what she wore under it.

But tonight was a fund-raiser, and some decorum was called for, so she chose the second one, still sleek and elegant, but a little tamer. A strapless sheath with a beaded lace shrug, it hinted but didn't advertise and had the added advantage of being Redstone red.

The color was a declaration. It had been too bold, too assertive for Daniel's taste, and he'd ordered her not to wear it. Since the functions she would have chosen it for were for his work, she hadn't fought him on it.

Looking back, of course, she realized it had been a glaring sign of what was to come.

But now she wore what she pleased when she pleased. And wearing Redstone red appealed to her on that level as well, not to mention that she was rarely alone; many in the Redstone family made a point of showing their loyalty in that subtle way.

And that it was a color that looked exceptionally well on her was something she didn't allow herself to dwell on when she chose it for tonight over the other options in her closet.

She simply wanted to look her best for the cause, she told herself. It had nothing to do with the man who would accompany her.

She glanced at the thin gold watch on her wrist; she'd dispensed with her daily, utilitarian model for a more delicate one, with a small diamond at the twelve and the six, unable to make the break completely and go without one at all.

The watch, a pair of drop earrings in gold set with a single ruby each, and a thin gold chain around her neck completed the outfit; she'd always followed her mother's rule of no more than three pieces of jewelry. Others in Daniel's circle had worn much more on such occasions, some simply dripping with the diamonds that shouted their status, and had given her pitying glances for her lack of flash and sparkle.

Daniel hadn't pitied her. He'd been angry. He'd tried varying tactics to get her to change her style, from buying her bigger and better jewels, to asking, to outright ordering her to put on more or flashier pieces. When she'd refused, he'd accused her of trying to undermine him by making it seem among their friends that he couldn't match their show.

And if they truly were our friends, she'd told herself then, the thought would never occur to them.

Looking back, she'd realized that had been another sign. At the time she'd just thought him silly—and exhausting—for making it a competition. But then, for a Huntington, everything was, even the games of tennis he played with a ferocity that made it seem close to a blood sport.

She doubted if Tony Alvera had ever had time for such frivolous things. A long weekend spent at a country club tennis tournament didn't seem like something he would indulge in, even if his world had included such things.

"Now, what do you know about it?" she told herself sternly. "Nothing. Josh sent him to college, perhaps he joined the tennis team."

Lord, she was talking to herself. Not the inner voice she guessed most people had, putting thoughts into words to aid in the process of working something out, but out loud, question-and-answer talking to herself about ridiculous things.

When the knock on her door came, it was a surprise. Not because she wasn't expecting it, although it was a few minutes early, but because instead of the heavy, demanding rapping she'd half anticipated, it was a firm but polite tapping.

And no cutesy rhythm, not for Tony Alvera.

Because this is all business, and you'd best remember that, she ordered herself as she walked through her living room to open the door.

When he'd been up the first time, to look at the wire across the stairs, he hadn't come inside. They'd been in a hurry to get to Chino before the favor Redstone had called in expired. This afternoon, he'd merely seen her to the door, as if he'd sensed she was already about at her limit at his insistence on following her home.

This time she supposed he would at least be stepping inside, so she glanced around, although she'd made certain it was tidy when she'd first gotten home.

Because you knew this would happen? Straightening up for the bodyguard, Lil?

She smiled in spite of herself as she realized she'd used Josh's nickname for her. He was one of the very few who ever shortened her name, although it didn't particularly bother her when someone did. In fact, she'd grown to like it, since it had once irritated Daniel, who had also insisted on being addressed by his full name rather than the detested Dan or worse, Danny.

It was with that smile on her face that she pulled the door open and, as she'd practiced in her head, gestured him inside.

If she hadn't done that mental practice, she likely would still be standing there, hand on the doorknob and her jaw hanging open in shock, she thought wryly a moment later.

Tony Alvera made her spacious living room seem small with his edgy presence. He made even her straightforward, low-key décor seem fussy compared to his lean, pared-down style in a perfectly fitted tux with a wing-collared shirt and classic bow tie—hand tied, she noted.

He also made the air seem a little thin, she thought as she finally remembered to breathe.

Something about the way he was looking at her made her think there would be no more air outside than there was in here.

"I came early to do a security check on your place," he said, his voice sounding oddly gruff.

So much for the niceties, Lilith thought. But in fact she was grateful for the businesslike approach. It took things out of the realm of the personal.

She had to admit that her first sight of Tony Alvera in a tux had blasted her imagination into some very personal areas.

And blasted the doting aunt analogy she'd been clinging to into an astronomical number of pieces.

Okay, so he was gorgeous, in a dark, exotic way that literally took her breath away. That was a fact, and no amount of calling herself a fool would change it. Any woman with a pulse would find it picking up at the sight of him.

And she had to walk into a crowded room with him tonight. With every woman in the place no doubt wondering what he was doing with *her* when he could have one of them—younger, more innocent and baggage free—with one snap of his elegant fingers.

None of them, of course, would be wondering what she was doing with him. One look at him in that tux would make that question irrelevant.

She fought for control, while he seemed briskly professional as he checked all the windows in the living room, looking at locks, trying to open them both locked and unlocked and peering out through them, she guessed to check possible access.

She didn't know him well enough—and he'd said nothing

more than those few words of explanation—to know if that odd note in his voice meant anything.

Perhaps he didn't want to be doing this—going to this thing with her—anymore than she did.

She steeled herself, wondering what had happened to all her vaunted determination and resolve. Get over yourself, Lil, she muttered inwardly.

"I'm sorry you had to do the penguin suit," she said, trying to break the tension even as she wasn't sure she wasn't the only one feeling it.

He glanced at her as he headed toward the next room, the smaller den that served as her home office, his expression unreadable.

"It's just another disguise," he said, and kept going.

She wasn't sure what that was supposed to mean. Clearly he wasn't happy about being here, so she decided his was the best approach and kept things on topic from then on.

"No windows in the den," she pointed out.

He nodded, and indeed his check in there was quicker. Then came the small dining room, the same routine as in the living room for the single large window. The kitchen took longer; there was a sunny garden window in the breakfast nook, with sliding panels that opened for venting, and he frowned until he walked over and saw there was no easy way to access it from outside.

When he then headed down the hall toward the bedrooms, she realized with a jolt what he was going to find if he stuck his nose in the master bathroom. She'd left it quite a mess, including some sexy underwear she'd firmly decided against wearing, which she now wished she had put back in the drawer instead of leaving it until she got home.

Stirred now, she followed him as he opened the door to her only occasionally used guest room. If he was bemused by the bunk beds and animated character décor—her young niece and nephew were the most frequent occupants of the room—he didn't show it. He merely walked over to the single window, again checked the lock and looked out, then came back.

And headed toward the last remaining rooms, the master suite.

At least I made the bed this morning.

Not that it seemed it mattered; as he walked over to the sliding glass door that led to the balcony, he didn't even glance at the big, white, cottage-style bed she'd bought as compensation for living for so long with Daniel's heavier, darker tastes.

In fact, he seemed to be studiously avoiding looking at it, she thought. Which obviously had to be a silly assumption on her part, there was no reason—

"This won't work," he said.

No, it won't, she thought. She was having no luck at all in her effort to ignore the effect this dangerously elegant man was having on her, no matter how silly or ridiculous she told herself she was being.

But she hadn't expected him to say it, especially so baldly.

"That balcony is too easy to get to, from above or the side. You need something more secure than this lock."

For an instant she was more grateful than she'd ever been in her life that his back was to her.

"I do?" she asked, figuring she could manage the two simple syllables without giving away her stupidity; when she heard the slight quaver in her voice she knew she should have kept quiet.

He didn't miss it, either. He turned his head, his gaze narrowed as he looked at her. With one of the greater efforts of her life, she steadied herself.

"You mean like a burglar bar? I've been meaning to do that." She was proud of how she sounded that time. Business-like, cool, calm. Herself.

After a second he shook his head, apparently deciding he'd imagined whatever he thought he'd heard in her voice. Or in answer to her question, she wasn't sure which.

"No. Those are useless against a pro. He'll just pop this little hook lock and lift the whole door out of the track. I'll get a pin for it, put it in tomorrow."

"A pin?"

He pointed to the top of the slider, where the moving panel and the stationary panel overlapped at the center. "You drill a hole through both frames. Put a heavy steel pin through both. Then you can't lift the door out or open it."

"Oh. What if I want to open it?"

"It's on a short chain fastened to the frame, so you can take it out and not lose it. But," he added, "don't."

"Don't what?"

"Open the door."

She blinked. "Don't open the door?"

"Don't open it. Get some pots or something, put them all along that railing, so anybody coming over will have to make noise. Then stay off the balcony. In fact, stay away from this—" he gestured at the expanse of glass "—altogether."

"Excuse me?" Irritation was starting to spark in her now. She'd been tolerant so far, but this was starting to go over the top.

"You heard me. Stay away from all the windows, and at night keep your lights to a minimum or curtains and blinds closed."

He couldn't know the nerve he was hitting, she told herself. But that didn't stop her from lifting her head and resorting to her most imperious voice. "I beg your pardon, but are you implying that I should become a prisoner in my own home, and in the dark as well?"

"No."

"Well, that's a relief," she muttered.

"I wasn't implying at all. I was ordering."

That did it. She drew herself up to her full height—and augmented by three-inch heels, she was a respectable five foot eight, only four or so inches shorter than he.

"I'm sorry," she said coolly, "but I quit taking orders from anyone in my personal life the day I left my husband. And you," she added sourly, "are beginning to sound a bit too much like him."

He went still. Something flashed in his dark eyes, something hot, grim and dangerous. It was all she could do not to take a step back from him.

"I am," he said, his voice low and harsh, "*nothing* like your ex-husband."

No, he wasn't, Lilith thought, regretting her words. Tony would never take out his anger or frustration on someone weaker than he. She opened her mouth to apologize, but he'd already turned and walked away. She told herself she should be thankful; at least he'd blown her silly thoughts right out of her mind.

As she stood there, watching him go, she wondered where she'd gotten the idea that he'd meant much more than just that.

Chapter 11

"I didn't do it!"

It was the standard, instinctive answer of any kid who was caught doing something he shouldn't have done. Tony knew that. It had never done him much good as a kid; with him, his father had operated on the assumption of guilty until proven innocent.

Lucy, on the other hand, had been able to get away with almost anything simply by giving their father that look, those big brown eyes turned on him liked a beaten puppy. The old man would just melt. Tony had tried hard to be mad at her for it, but she had used it on him as well, and he hadn't been immune.

And ever since she'd been killed, he'd been hard pressed to be tough on a kid. Any kid. But he had to be a little tougher on this one. Until he was sure.

"I didn't do it, honest!" Billy Wells exclaimed again when Tony didn't immediately respond. "I heard my mom talking about how she fell, and I came up here to see if Lilith was okay."

"And why," he said, purposefully stepping close enough so that he towered over the nine-year-old, "should I believe you?"

"Because it's the truth!" Billy looked up at him, and the fear in his eyes was real. "I did that other stuff, the fire and the flat tires, but I didn't do that! Mrs. Tilly is a grumpy old bi—bag, but I like Lilith. She's nice to me, and my mom. I wouldn't try to hurt her."

He believed him. Whether it was the fear, or the urgency in his quavering voice, Tony believed him. But that didn't mean a warning wasn't in order, given the boy's admissions to other questionable actions.

"I'm going to find out who did," he said. "And if I find out you had anything to do with it, you're going to see me again, and you won't like it."

"I didn't," the boy insisted for the third time, but more calmly now. Then, as if sensing the immediate crisis had passed, he looked at Tony with a touch of curiosity. "You a cop or something?"

"Or something," he said, wondering about the change, wondering what had given the kid that kind of knowledge. "I work for Lilith's boss."

"Oh. That Redstone guy? My mom says he's a bazillionaire."

"Probably."

"Wish he'd give us some of it."

"He gives it to people who work hard to earn it."

The boy frowned. "Not to people who need it?"

"If they're willing to work for it. Then he'll help more than anybody you'll ever meet."

"Maybe my mom could go to work for him. She works hard. She's got like three jobs."

Tony's brow furrowed. "That's a lot."

"She's always tired. And worried. If she could get just one good job, then we could stay here, and not have to move all the time."

Tony heard a female voice call the boy's name. Billy's head turned, and he spoke quickly.

"I gotta go. I promised I'd be back in five minutes. She gets worried if I'm late. Like my dad could ever find us here."

Then he was scampering down the stairs, leaving Tony pondering those last words. It didn't take much to guess what was behind them. No wonder Lilith was considering getting his mother hired at Redstone. He could put in a word himself, he thought, even as he realized he was grasping for distraction from the night ahead, something he was anticipating with an odd sense of eagerness and dreading at the same time.

But his belief that the boy had been telling the truth also meant he was facing the greater possibility that Josh was right; if the boy hadn't strung that wire across this landing, if it hadn't been a childish prank that could have turned lethal, then the chances that someone was truly after Lilith rose dramatically.

And his gut-deep reaction to that put him even more on edge.

A few minutes later, when Lilith came out her door and he saw the way that damned red dress moved when she did, when they got down to his car and he watched her get in, saw the slim ankles above the red shoes she wore, imagined how her legs must look in those spiky heels, he knew the confused feelings were appropriate.

He was not, Tony thought, going to make it through this night. A night of rich, sophisticated, high-society types, and most of them would probably be gaping at him and Lilith, wondering what on earth a classy lady like her was doing with a guy like him.

Probably figure I'm after her money, he thought. And the fact that thanks to Harlan McClaren, one of Josh's first investors and the canniest financial adviser on the West Coast, he'd never have another money worry in his life, didn't change that. He still looked the way he looked, and he was going to stand out in this crowd like a wolf in the flock.

If it wasn't for Josh…

But it was. This was all for Josh, so he had no choice. That's how he had to look at this. It was for Josh, and therefore imperative. He'd shut off his feelings before, often, so he would do the same now. And he would handle this as if it were nothing more than any other security assignment.

It would work, he thought. As long as he never looked at the woman now sitting beside him in the car.

It had taken everything he had in him not to grab her and kiss her when she'd opened the door, standing there in that long column of vibrant red. Not the sexy number she'd worn to the Christmas party the first time he'd seen her, but an elegant, shimmering strapless dress with a lacy, short, jacket-thing over it that sparkled with crystals or something.

This was closer to the real Lilith, he supposed. He wondered if she realized what a dichotomy the two presented: the sexy, slinky, low cut dress, and this stylish, tasteful, screamingly chic gown. This was the cool, unflappable Lilith, untouchable in his mind.

Untouchable, except that that was the first thing he'd wanted to do. Touch. And more. A lot more.

The atmosphere in the car was a little tense. His fault, he thought, he'd snapped at her, and for no good reason. She had every right to be upset at this invasion of her privacy.

Not to mention your high-handed orders, he told himself ruefully.

He'd overreacted. Again. He'd been reeling from the sight of her, and when he'd seen the vulnerabilities in her home and visualized the worst happening to her, he'd gone over the top in addressing them.

And her.

But when she'd said that about him being like her ex, he'd lost it. And ironically, it wasn't even the comparison to a wife beater that hit him so hard; he knew it wasn't anywhere close to true, and he knew on some level that Lilith knew it as well.

It was every other way it wasn't true that hit him. He truly wasn't anything like Daniel Huntington. He wasn't smooth, suave, sophisticated, polished or anything someone born to the manor as Huntington had been was. Oh, he could act it, and put on a pretty good front, but that's all it was, an act. Underneath he was still Tonio from the streets, and he was beginning to think he always would be.

And now he had to walk into a roomful of people just like Huntington—hopefully most without his particular predilections—and pretend he belonged.

And he had to do it with the woman who personified that world to him. Also pretending he belonged.

Something, he realized, he hadn't explained to her yet. At least he was driving, so he didn't have to look at her. He drew in a deep breath and took the plunge.

"Since I've already made you so angry, I might as well finish the job. We have to talk about tonight."

"I'm not angry."

He flicked her a sideways glance. "You could have fooled me."

"Oh, I was angry. But it was a reflex, an old reflex I thought I was over. You didn't deserve it, you were only doing your job. That I feel that job is unnecessary is irrelevant. I'm sorry."

It was as pretty an apology as he'd ever gotten. And he had no idea what to say. Her ex probably would. He'd accept gracefully, charmingly and everything would be smoothed over with consummate skill.

Finally, he decided the only thing he could do was talk normally, as if they'd reverted to the time before tonight, and hope she'd understand. "Think of it as Homeland Security on a smaller scale. Parts are annoying, but the final result is safety."

He sensed her looking at him, but had to negotiate a turn.

"Interesting analogy," was all she said, but in the slightly more relaxed tone of her voice he read her understanding of his unspoken acceptance of her apology. For a moment silence spun out, until she asked, "What about tonight?"

He'd almost forgotten. And now he had to hit her with something that would likely be even more annoying than the orders given for her security.

"We—Redstone Security, I mean—try to maintain a very low profile," he said.

"I know," she said. "I know you try to keep interaction even inside Redstone to a minimum, in case you have to work on the inside."

He nodded. "Good thing bad apples at Redstone are about as rare as five-leaf clovers. You're cleaning up after the only one ever found at Headquarters."

"I know. But it must be exciting, to travel all over the world. Redstone is just about everywhere, in some form."

"It has its moments."

"Liana told me you returned only a few months ago from a job in Rio de Janeiro."

Beck, he thought. What was it about love that made you turn into a fount of information you normally wouldn't share with anyone?

"Yes," he said.

"She said you cleaned up a mess that even Draven had doubts that one man could handle."

"Logan Beck talks too much."

She laughed, and suddenly he understood why the ex-cop couldn't seem to keep anything from his redheaded siren. Who wouldn't say anything to keep a laugh like that coming?

"So, what about tonight?"

"That low profile means that tonight, I'm not Redstone Security."

"All right," she said.

He waited, silently, for her to get the point.

"What are you, then?"

He knew she was smart; hell, he knew she was damn near brilliant, so it had to be just that the possibility would never in a million years occur to her. He couldn't blame her. On appearances alone it was likely no one would believe it. A classy, pure lady like Lilith Mercer with a street thug like him?

"And to think I could have been an accountant, wrestling with spreadsheets instead of this," he muttered.

"You?" She almost yelped it. "An accountant?"

"Is that so impossible?" He wasn't sure whether to be offended or not. "I have a perfectly good business degree."

It must have sounded in his voice, because she hastened to say, "Oh, please. It's just that I can't picture you being happy behind a desk."

Since he'd used the same argument with Josh when he'd asked for the chance at Redstone Security, he felt his irritation fade.

"I wasn't. I tried, for nearly a year. In Marketing and Distribution, like a good little worker bee." He grimaced. "Don't get me wrong, that office at Redstone is a lot better than most places, but it just…"

"Wasn't you," she finished. "I can't imagine you being anything but miserable."

"I was. But I thought I owed it to Josh."

She shifted in her seat then. "All anyone he's helped ever owes Josh is to make the absolute most of the chance he's given them. That's all he ever wants or expects."

"I know. Now. Then I thought I was letting him down."

She was quiet for a moment. "I'm guessing he figured out how unhappy you were."

He flicked a glance at her again. She was smiling, knowing as all of Redstone did, what came first with their boss.

"Yes, he did." He turned his attention back to the road. "He asked what I really wanted. I told him."

"And thus a match made in heaven."

He didn't dare look at her again. "Something like that."

"And you've been happy?"

"Yes." Except when it cost someone I was just falling in love with her life.

That the feelings he'd had then were minuscule compared to what he was feeling now was something he didn't want to think about, didn't dare think about, not now.

And they still hadn't gotten to it. They had, however, reached the hotel where the gala was to be held.

"Sorry I can't have the valets park it," he said as he turned away from the booth outside the hotel lobby. "There are some things in this car we wouldn't want the hassle of explaining. All with permits, but convincing the police of that would be…time-consuming."

She merely nodded. He found a spot, parked, shut the car off, then turned in the driver's seat to look at her.

"Tonight," he began, determined to finish it now.

"You're not security," she repeated dutifully. "So what are you?"

"Your date."

She stared at him. To his chagrin, color flooded her face. He heard her take a quick, deep breath. Obviously he'd shocked her, although he couldn't help thinking she should have seen this as the most logical approach.

Her reaction needled him, and for the second time tonight he overreacted, knowing he was doing it even as he spoke.

"Or," he said, drawing the words out and accompanying them with the smile of invitation he used only when working, "if you'd rather, your lover."

Chapter 12

Lilith told herself it was her imagination, that not everyone in the room was going quiet and staring at them, but she was having trouble convincing herself when heads kept turning.

She was still a little breathless from that moment in the car when Tony had uttered the words that had stolen her breath in the first place.

She'd felt hot and cold and tangled inside, and only years of practice had allowed her to face him with any semblance of calm and ask levelly, "And just how should I introduce you?"

"Antonio Diego Alvera Bernard," he'd said, throwing the name out as if it were some sort of challenge.

As, perhaps, it was.

Now that they were inside and walking through the ballroom, she realized she was so off-balance from what he'd said that she was probably acting exactly as he'd wanted her to. And was fairly sure that had been his plan—to make her act like a woman out for an evening with a lover, perhaps a new one, on edge and a little uncertain. Which, she knew, was how most people would interpret the tension between them.

Except for those wondering what a guy like Tony Alvera was doing with a woman old enough to be…

She'd forgotten the demise of her doting aunt analogy, and she wasn't sure what to put in its place.

A woman old enough to be very foolish will probably do nicely, she told herself sternly.

If she'd known this was going to be the approach tonight, that they would be masquerading as two people on a formal date, she would have had time to think of what to say. But she hadn't, so now she had to think on the fly. The temptation to just play up the facade, to play it as if it were true, to act as if there was truly something between them, was so incredibly tempting that she knew it was dangerous.

…if you'd rather, your lover.

She felt a sudden rush of heat, and feared she must be as red as her dress.

"Lilith! You look wonderful."

She turned to see Alicia Cramer, a woman she knew from the organization this fund-raiser was for. The woman was a five-foot powerhouse who had done more to bring research money into the field than anyone except Josh himself, and for that Lilith was willing to overlook her somewhat haughty manner. Most of the time.

But right now she was eyeing Tony Alvera like a person who'd just seen something impossible. True, she had always come to this function alone, in fact had never brought anyone who wasn't a business relationship or someone she'd hoped would respond to the fund-raising aspect of the evening, but there was much more to Alicia's avidly curious inspection.

And so it begins, she thought.

"Alicia, how are you?" she said with every evidence of delight, hoping her tone would foster reality.

"I'm fine, thank you," Alicia said, but she was still eyeing Tony. And there was a hint of doubt in her gaze, something that wasn't quite puzzlement and wasn't quite distrust, but some combination leavened with a touch of fear that made Lilith feel defensive. She looked as if she were wondering if someone had left a door open somewhere, letting him wander in off the street.

As if, Lilith thought, he wasn't the hottest man in the room. The defensiveness sparked.

"Meet Antonio Diego Alvera Bernard," she said, rolling out his full name grandly and purposefully making her voice sound as if she were introducing visiting royalty.

Then she waited; Alicia was too smoothly polished to be rude, but Lilith expected at the least an arched brow as she contemplated the unlikely couple they made.

If Tony was surprised at her deferential introduction, he didn't let it show. Instead he played along with her perfectly, took the uncertain woman's hand and gave her a courtly bow.

"My deepest pleasure, madame," he said, in a formal voice and an old-world inflection Lilith had never heard from him. "It is an honor to be here on such a worthwhile occasion."

To Lilith's amazement, the supercilious Alicia actually blushed.

Why are you surprised? she asked herself. He's made you blush more than once. But for, she had to admit ruefully, very different reasons.

Or maybe not, she thought as she watched him work on Alicia as if she were any woman he'd set out to charm. His reputation in that arena was clearly well earned. Lilith remembered Liana's frequent jokes about the fact that all Tony's sources in official places seemed to be female. Now that she was seeing him in action firsthand, she understood why.

Which set her to wondering why he hadn't used the charm he obviously had in abundance on her. Not that she would be susceptible to it; she'd learned to distrust charm the hard way.

But he hadn't even tried to beguile her into cooperating with him. He'd just ordered. Arrogantly.

Of course, she worked for Redstone. Not that that stopped him from, however teasingly, exercising that charm on, say, Liana, even though her love for Logan Beck made her immune. And that had also been during a Redstone assignment, so that wasn't the difference, either.

Perhaps he just saved the charm for women closer to his own age. But then, he'd just turned it on full bore for Alicia, who was at least sixty-five.

So maybe it's just you, she thought.

She nearly laughed at the glumness of her own thought; she normally wasn't given to such absurdities. It was, she knew, most likely a combination of factors, probably including the fact that she apparently had the ability to make him angry. Why, she didn't know, but assumed it was because he knew this was a lot of wasted time, that no one was really out to get her, and while he was tied up doing this, no doubt agents dealing with real, serious situations for Redstone could be using his help.

But what she also didn't know, and what unsettled her even more, was why this even mattered to her. Now, *that,* she told herself, was the height of absurdity.

"Lilith?"

She snapped back to the present with such a jolt she thought it must have been obvious to everyone. Fortunately, while she'd been lost in silly contemplation, Alicia had moved on, obviously deciding against evicting the dangerous-looking man Lilith had brought into their midst. The man who was looking at her curiously.

"That effortless charm of yours is amazing," she said, hoping he hadn't read her foolish thoughts in her face.

"That *charm,*" he snapped, startling her, "is effortless because it's meaningless. I learned it just like I learned what fork to use. I honed it because it worked. It's as put on as this—" he tugged at one lapel of the expensive tuxedo "—is. I'm a fake, hadn't you realized?"

Lilith stared at him; clearly she'd finally hit a nerve. That it was this surprised her. Could he really think that learning such skills late made them any less real? Could he—

"Lilith!"

She turned at the hail, and found herself face-to-face with Grace O'Conner Draven.

True pleasure rang in her voice as she exclaimed, "Grace!"

The two women hugged genuinely. She hadn't seen Grace much since the wedding. Not only was she still one of Redstone's most important cogs, designer and builder of airstrips all over the world, but she had become a frequent spokeswoman for the Back to Life Foundation that was the beneficiary of tonight's fund-raiser.

As one of the first recipients of Ian Gamble's incredible prosthetic foot, she was the perfect choice. No one who looked at the slender, lovely woman with the short, wispy dark hair and the vivid blue eyes would ever guess she'd been through such hell. Trapped by tons of debris after a violent earthquake in Turkey, her right foot crushed beyond repair, Grace had survived. She'd hung on long enough for the man who would eventually become her husband to reach her.

And she'd survived what he'd had to do to her to save her life.

Of course, Lilith knew there were those who would say that being married to John Draven would require more courage than either of those. Lilith wasn't one of them; from the first time she'd seen them together she'd known they had what she'd never had, that magical, incredible connection of two people completely right for each other and deeply in love.

"Mrs. Draven." Tony spoke in that formal tone again, yet this time it was laced with a respect that made it sound very different than when he'd spoken to Alicia Cramer. Of course, this was the wife of his boss, the head of Redstone Security.

And Lilith realized he'd waited until there was no one in earshot to speak, no one to hear that he knew who she was. And that he addressed her by her married name, something only those inside Redstone ever used. To the world she was still Grace O'Conner, out of the need to keep her husband's position at Redstone as low profile as possible.

"Mr. Alvera," Grace answered, a teasing glint in her eyes. "My, but you do clean up nice."

Doesn't he just? Lilith muttered inwardly.

Before her thoughts could spin out of control again, there were others there, and Tony and Grace both put on a show of just having met. Grace obviously realized—or perhaps she knew, given whom she shared pillow talk with—that he was working, and had quickly caught on that he was here undercover. Lilith knew Draven would never share details of an ongoing investigation, but he was madly, crazily in love with his wife, and Grace was a smart, perceptive woman.

"And don't you two make a couple?" Grace added.

Lilith blinked. She sensed Tony going very still. Grace went on cheerfully.

"You so golden, him so dark, and both gorgeous. It's hardly fair to us ordinary folk. I don't know who people are going to think got lucky," Grace added with a teasing smile.

More likely they'll wonder how much I had to pay the young stud to escort me, Lilith thought dryly.

She tried to mentally slap herself for the thought. She knew she was attractive enough, and that people rarely believed she was in her mid-forties. She told herself her uncertainty about her personal appeal was a legacy from Daniel that she needed to be rid of, but that was easier said than done.

"I'd guess," Tony was saying easily, "they're all simply wondering why a classy, uptown lady like her is with a reprobate like me."

Grace snorted inelegantly, rolling her eyes at him. "Oh,

please. I can't speak for the males in the room, but no woman on the planet will wonder that."

Lilith barely stopped herself from echoing the opinion, since she'd thought it herself just minutes ago. She envied Grace her ease with the man, and supposed it stemmed from the fact that he worked for her husband. She probably knew him much better than Lilith did, although Lilith couldn't help wondering if anyone really knew this man.

When Grace walked away moments later, toward the raised dais where she would make her impassioned speech for the support of the foundation—and if asked, not hesitate to lift the hem of her sleek, blue satin dress to show the prosthetic foot that had, in its way, brought her here tonight—Tony spoke as if that moment of oddly still tension had never occurred.

"Anyone who didn't know would be stunned to learn she'd lost a foot."

"Which is," Lilith said, responding to his normal tone with the best one she could manage, "the point of the evening. Ian's work in prosthetics is cutting edge, and Josh will fund him endlessly, but getting the prosthetics to people who need them is what the Back to Life Foundation does best."

"Sounds like you could be up there touting," Tony observed.

"I could," Lilith said. "I have. Grace is a good friend, and I admire her. She makes this issue personal for me."

"And personal makes you passionate."

She didn't think he meant it as a double entendre but didn't dare look at him to find out. "Yes," she said simply.

And with that she pulled herself together and began to do what she was here for, to work the room. As a representative of Redstone, she knew her job; in a way she was working as much here as she did in her office.

But as she went around the room, greeting those she knew warmly, encouraging them to be even more generous than last year, greeting strangers even more warmly, welcoming them to this chance to make a difference, she couldn't help but be aware of the frequent looks they were garnering. She would have assumed the stares were for all the reasons she'd expected them, but Grace's words made her wonder now.

She introduced Tony by name only—forgoing now the full, grand introduction she'd given him to the haughty Alicia—and he took it from there. He was, it quickly became clear, quite capable of handling himself in this setting, of turning on that easy charm, although to her it didn't quite mask the edgy hyperalertness.

But after a while Lilith quit worrying and became almost amused at the way women responded with blushing pleasure and fascination, and men reacted with a wariness usually accompanied by a furrow between the eyebrows, as if they weren't sure this man was quite domesticated.

Occasionally she caught women—some she knew, some she didn't—glancing at her with an expression that was unmistakably envious.

...no woman on the planet will wonder...

No, Lilith thought, she didn't suppose they would. And as she gave him a sideways look, saw that unexpected dimple flash as he made another of his courtly bows, noticed yet again how devastatingly attractive he was in that perfectly fitted tux, how he managed to exude that charm and yet never lose that edginess, she caught herself wishing, for just the tiniest moment, that it was real.

Chapter 13

Tony smothered a yawn. He was on his third cup of coffee and it wasn't even nine o'clock yet. This did not bode well.

As he waited in the back of the small bodega, watching people—mostly older women or young ones with children in tow picking up groceries; later it would be men who migrated to the wine shop along one side—come and go, he tried to distract himself by remembering when he had come to this place himself, running errands for his mother. It didn't work.

He shook his head in an effort to clear it, knowing he was walking a dangerous line. The combination of endless tension and tiredness was hardly the best for someone in his line of work.

But sleep had not been in the cards for him again last night. In fact, he hadn't had much sleep since that blasted charity fund-raiser on Tuesday night. It was crazy, it made no sense, but going in there as Lilith's date, knowing everyone other than Grace and perhaps a few others from Redstone assumed they were together as a couple, had somehow changed everything.

And it wasn't simply that his imagination had run amok, leaping from what he guessed they were thinking to his own seemingly uncontrollable fantasies. It was more that he wanted them not to be fantasies. He wanted what everyone in that room was thinking to be true. He wanted their assumptions that when he and Lilith left that glittering affair, they would do it together, that wherever they went back to, it would be together, that when they went to bed, it would be together.

Need cramped him up yet again, and he fought it with the grim determination he'd learned at a very early age. But at that age, he hadn't known this kind of need even existed.

And he certainly never, ever would have pictured himself feeling like this over a woman like Lilith Mercer.

He should, he knew now, never have taken this assignment. When she'd been safely out of his sphere, he'd been able to deal, able to laugh at himself for his ridiculous feelings for a woman so far out of his reach. But now, now that he'd spent days with her constantly in his mind if not always his presence, that barrier of distance was shattered, and he didn't know if he could ever rebuild it.

That he would have to, he knew. Somehow. And sooner rather than later, since there hadn't been a trace of a problem since the trip wire four days ago.

When his cell phone had signaled a text message early this morning, he'd been getting ready to go pick Lilith up at her condo—and postponing figuring out exactly what was going to happen this weekend. At least for today and tomorrow she would be tucked safely inside Redstone Headquarters for the day; he hadn't even dared to ask if she had plans for the weekend.

A sudden vision of himself playing bodyguard to Lilith on a date with some nebulous upper-crust type slammed into him, making him feel as if he'd taken a roundhouse punch to the gut. He had to fight for breath, stunned at his own reaction.

The image played out. Dinner, maybe a movie, Lilith in that

sexy red number from the Christmas party—never mind that it was hardly something she'd wear out on an ordinary night—that unknown man who looked too much like her ex-husband holding her hand as they watched some chick flick that would inspire them to go home and reenact the love scenes….

How the hell do I keep from killing the guy?

He shook his head again, this time at least dispelling the remnants of the video loop his sleep-deprived brain insisted on running. He knew he was in trouble when he was thinking of murdering some imagined character that might not even exist.

The last time he'd felt anything like this, Lisa had died. And what he'd felt then hadn't had the chance to become what he was feeling now.

He made himself focus. Although there had been no sign or mention of a man in her life, he simply couldn't picture a woman like Lilith not having them constantly buzzing around her like flies.

Or fluttering, like that pompous, deceptively pretty butter fly Huntington.

He used those images, the memory of how the man had spoken to her, to jab himself back to the matter at hand. With a glance at his watch, he wondered if Rico was going to show up at all.

The text message this morning had simply told him to be here by nine. More accurately, it had said only, *La Bodega—9:00 a.m.* The implication being, of course, that Rico had something to tell him.

Or maybe it's a setup, he thought. *Maybe they're finally coming after me to show me how you don't ever really leave the neighborhood.*

He knew he was tired when he started having paranoid ideas like that. If they'd wanted him dead, he would have been long ago. But he'd never really been that active in the ES 13s, he'd pulled his stunt with Josh before he'd gotten in too deep. In fact, that stunt had been a sort of proving ground dare, to find some rich guy and rip him off, bringing the proceeds back to Chaco, who at the time was the leader.

Now he was in Pelican Bay, doing the hardest of hard time for killing three civilians and two cops in a shoot-out during a drug bust gone bad.

One of those civilians had been fifteen-year-old Lucinda Alvera.

Maybe that was why they'd let him go, Tony thought, taking a final sip of the coffee that was now cooled to lukewarm. They understood death and what it meant. Most of them had lost somebody, many of them somebody they'd loved as he'd loved Lucy.

He tossed the cup into the wastebasket beside him. The irony of that possibility, that Lucy's life had been the price of his ticket out, bit deep and hard, and his jaw clenched.

He'd just decided he'd had enough of hanging around this place that was haunted for him when the front door opened again, the jingle of the old-fashioned bell attached to it a cheerful sound amid the grim recollections. He looked that way.

Rico.

With the swagger typical of ES 13s, he called out an over-exuberant greeting to old man Martinez, who watched the gangster warily as he walked toward the back of the bodega. But, Tony noticed, the bluster vanished and Rico looked around carefully before he approached.

"You owe me a coat, man."

"If it's worth it, you got it." Tony cut to the chase. "What?"

"One of my guys, Carlito, he knows a guy who knows a guy who—"

"I don't need the history. Just give it to me."

"That's the problem with people these days, y'know? No respect for the rituals."

"Plenty of respect," Tony said. "No time. You want money in the pocket of that coat, *digame.*"

At the order to just tell him, Rico shrugged. "A guy did time in Chino. Cell mate with a guy who did time with a guy—"

He stopped when Tony's gaze narrowed, then shrugged again and went on. "End of the string is some guy in one of those lightweight places, you know? Private, minimum security? Out in Baker. He knew some guy there who used to work for that place, Redstone. He talked a lot about payback, for them putting him in jail. Mentioned some woman who took his place."

Tony nearly stopped breathing.

"That your friend's ex?" Rico asked.

"Could be," Tony said, keeping it vague. "I'm not sure what she does. This guy got a name?" he asked, although he knew perfectly well who it had to be.

"My friend, he says it's Stan. Don't know any more than that."

Stan Chilton. The ramifications started to rapid-fire in Tony's mind, and he had to yank himself back to the present. "I need to talk to this friend of yours."

Rico pondered this for a moment, and Tony guessed he was considering just how much payment he could push for.

"Could be arranged."

"You just earned yourself a coat," Tony said. "With enough to buy another one in the pocket."

Rico laughed. "Don't need two coats, man. Lots better things to spend it on."

"Keep going," Tony said. "You find me more, you'll be able to buy a lot of them."

Rico grinned. "I find out more, I want that fancy car you drive, *mijo*."

Tony laughed, but his mind was already racing ahead. This turned everything around. If the person behind this was Stan Chilton, the former head of Redstone R&D, who had left in ignominy after being caught selling Ian Gamble's exclusive research, then the whole complexion of this had changed.

As soon as he was back in his car he would make the first call to Draven, using the hands-free Bluetooth system so he could be on his way to Redstone Headquarters at the same time. It suddenly seemed imperative that he get there as soon as he could.

Lilith was going to have to take this more seriously now; for the first time there was something more, however tenuous, than simply Josh's innate worry about his people. There was outside evidence that someone truly had it in for her, and while hearsay wasn't admissible in a courtroom, it was more than enough for Tony Alvera when it came to Lilith's safety.

He whipped the Redstone car quickly away from the curb as the phone rang on the other end. As he waited for Draven to answer, he found himself grimacing as he faced a thought he didn't want to analyze just yet but couldn't deny, either.

He'd been a lot happier when he'd been convinced the person behind the threat to Lilith was her ex-husband.

Chapter 14

"It's about ten times removed from firsthand hearsay," Tony said.

John Draven looked at him and nodded. "I got that."

"I'm just saying," Tony said, a bit uncomfortable under his boss's steady scrutiny.

"I know."

"It made more sense that it was her ex," he said, wondering if it sounded as lame as he felt it did. "Why would Chilton go after her? It's not like she had anything to do with him going to prison. She just came in to clean up the mess he left behind."

"If Chilton was man enough to come after the ones who really put him where he was, which would be Sam and Ian and me, he probably wouldn't have done what he did in the first place."

Tony couldn't argue with that cogent and concise argument, so didn't even try. "My contact's going to set up a meet with the guy who was in the slam with Chilton. Later today, I hope. I'll see if I can get any more."

Draven nodded. And then, in a way that even Tony knew

never would have happened before his marriage to Grace, he went on, almost conversationally. "Come in handy sometimes, those contacts."

It struck Tony, not for the first time, that it was rather amazing that Draven hadn't had using those contacts in mind from the moment he'd found out about him. In need of the distraction, he asked his boss something he'd always wondered.

"When you dug into my background sixteen years ago, how hard did you push Josh to toss me back where I belonged?"

Draven's legendary cool didn't waver. "Josh never asked me to do a background check on you."

"But you did," Tony said; he knew his boss well enough by now to know that unless directly ordered not to, Draven checked out everyone that might have access to *his* boss.

Draven's mouth twitched. "Of course."

"So?"

"I didn't. It's who Josh is, and it's not my place or desire to change that." He gave Tony a sideways look before adding, "I did push him to just give you that hand up, then let you sink or swim on your own."

"But when I finished school he took me into Redstone instead."

"I knew he would. I also knew you wouldn't be happy at a desk job, no matter how much business or accounting they crammed into your head."

"But you didn't figure I'd end up working for you someday, did you, *jefe?*"

Draven gave a one-shouldered shrug. "Josh is the real boss. I do what he wants."

Then, after a silent moment reminiscent of the old Draven, the onetime man of fewer words than anybody at Redstone except St. John, he again elaborated. "I didn't want you here just because of where you came from."

Tony's brow furrowed at the ambiguity of the statement. "You didn't want me because of that, or not *only* because of that?"

Draven's mouth twitched again. "Yes," he said. "The first because I thought that if I ever needed to send you back to the streets on a case, you might lose everything you'd gained."

Startled, Tony blinked. He'd heard the legends, of course, about this man before he'd ever come to work for him. You didn't work at Redstone long in any capacity before you heard about the head of the most famous and efficient private, company-run security team in the world. One of those legends—one Tony suspected was true—had both Josh and Draven approached by governments from various countries about privately contracting out for official security, but turning down the lucrative offers; they were Redstone, and that was enough.

The rest were the more common kind of thing, that Draven had more than once made a suspect confess just by the simple fact of his presence, that there was something in his eyes that made even the most brazen of bad guys quiver. Tony believed it; some combination of where he'd been, what he'd done and what he'd seen made him the most intimidating man he'd ever encountered, and he'd encountered a few on the streets of L.A.

But he'd always thought of Draven as focused strictly on that security; you didn't run a team as good as his, in as many places as Redstone had outposts around the world, without that kind of dedication.

But now it seemed Draven apparently subscribed to Josh's other doctrine as well—a hand up, not a hand out, to anyone willing to work for it.

"As for the other," Draven said, "I was afraid you'd be a loose cannon."

"And now?" Tony asked.

"You are a loose cannon," Draven said, and this time he grinned, a rare enough occurrence that it caught Tony off guard. "But I know you won't fire without just cause, so I don't worry about it much."

As a vote of confidence, Tony thought, it didn't come much

higher than that, not from John Draven. "You have Hill assigned to anything yet?"

"Not yet, it's been relatively quiet of late. You need her?"

"On call, maybe. In case that meeting comes up and I can't get back in time to see Lilith home."

Draven nodded. "I'll have her stand by."

"And stay with her until I get there."

Draven didn't ask, only nodded. And as he left the airport office of Redstone Security, Tony knew why.

Draven realized as well as he did now that the threat was real.

"Ms. Mercer?"

At the soft inquiry from the doorway, Lilith looked up, quashing a wince as her shoulder—and backside—reminded her of the tumble she'd taken.

A woman stood there, someone she'd never seen before, with straight, medium brown hair tied back and a quiet sort of face. Since Lilith knew almost everyone in the building that was odd, and if this was any place but Redstone she might worry that whatever threat she faced had found its way here.

But as she studied the plain, seemingly deferential figure before her, she couldn't imagine the woman doing anything in the least aggressive, let alone trying to hurt anyone. "Can I help you?"

"I'm Taylor Hill. Mr. Draven sent me. I'm here to see you home, whenever you're ready."

Automatically, Lilith glanced at the clock. It was a bit early for her to call it quits, although she'd been having trouble focusing this afternoon, ever since Tony had called her with the information he'd discovered about Stan Chilton.

She opened her mouth to ask where Tony was, but realized this young woman probably wouldn't know, anyway. Besides, she thought ruefully, with her luck lately, the question would come out sounding like a petulant whine.

She did wonder where he was, though. And with no small

qualm; it would hardly take a researcher—albeit that was pretty much what she was—to figure out that he hadn't come across the bit of information about Chilton at the local library.

She knew more about Tony now than she had; she'd rather delicately picked Liana's brain, knowing that Logan, and through him Liana, had to know a lot more than she did; she'd been merely a slightly involved bystander during the investigation of Logan's case. Tony had kept her in the loop, but their talks had been purely business.

Purely business, she thought again now. It struck her then that after that first day in her office, he'd never again turned upon her any of the oozing charm she'd seen him use to such effect on just about any other breathing female. Even Alicia, at the charity fund-raiser; if she hadn't seen it herself, she would have sworn the woman who'd been called a termagant more than once would be immune to such things.

The memory in turn made her think he'd been acting rather oddly ever since then. As if there were some kind of impenetrable wall between them.

Maybe that was why this woman was here instead. Not because Tony was busy, but because he didn't *want* to be here. Didn't want to be around her.

Perhaps he'd even asked to be taken off the case, she thought. Although now that it appeared there really *was* a case, that it wasn't just Josh's overprotectiveness, she found that hard to believe. Nobody who worked for Draven, or Josh, walked out in the middle of a job. Redstone simply didn't hire those kinds of people.

So she tried to find out, discreetly.

"Alvera afraid he's going to get sucked into another black-tie event?" she asked, with what she thought was a credible show of carefree good humor.

The woman never cracked a smile. "I wouldn't know, ma'am."

Ma'am.

Well, that put her solidly in her place, didn't it? Lilith thought. To this young thing, that's what she was. One foot in the grave. She refrained from asking Taylor how old she was. If her age started with a three rather than a two she'd be surprised.

Giving herself a mental shake, Lilith said briskly, "I won't be ready for a half hour or so, if you want to go find some coffee or something."

"That's fine. I'll be back in thirty minutes."

"On the dot," Lilith heard in her head, as if the young woman had said the words. Somehow she thought she probably would. If she'd said she needed thirty-two minutes, Taylor would have said and done exactly that. Lilith wondered what her story was. She'd have to ask Tony.

Assuming, of course, she ever saw him again.

Chapter 15

Alejandro "Loco" Degas wasn't going to be much more help, Tony thought. The man was of the sullen sort, marked by his life in ways that could never be changed. Since Tony guessed he was still under thirty, he'd apparently given up early. Not that he could blame him; at sixteen he'd been ready to give up himself, and if not for a knife, his own reckless decision and the intervention of Josh Redstone, he would have.

The only thing he'd gained from this meeting was the information that Chilton had apparently had help. Tony had figured that out himself already; Chilton didn't have the brains and hadn't been inside long enough to develop on his own the kind of network something like this would take. It was tougher to set up something like this in the minimum-security lockups, anyway; not many hit men or their ilk ended up there, unless they were undiscovered. In his experience, white-collar criminals, once they were caught, tended to crumple. They just weren't tough enough. Ruthless, yes, but prison tough? No.

Despite the lack of really solid information, he paid the man the agreed upon amount anyway and repeated the offer of more if anything else was turned up.

"I'm not a cop, and I don't have to go to court and prove any of this," he told both Degas and Rico, who had insisted on umpiring this meeting. "This is—" he almost stumbled and said the word *personal,* but recovered "—private, and even if it's second-hand hearsay or rumors, I want to hear it."

As he drove out of the neighborhood he'd once inhabited—he hesitated to say lived in—he wondered again if that help had been inside or outside. He wished he could somehow tie it back to Daniel Huntington, but Chino and the privately run minimum-security prison in Baker were different worlds as much as were these streets and the kinder, gentler streets of Bel Air or Beverly Hills.

Of course, Lilith wouldn't be happy if he did that.

And there it was again, just that quickly, eating at him, gnawing at a sore place somewhere inside him that no amount of effort could let him ignore.

She'd been relieved that it hadn't been her ex-husband.

At first, he'd tried to tell himself he'd imagined her reaction; after all, he'd told her over the phone about Chilton, he hadn't been there to see her face. But he knew, with every ounce of that gut instinct he'd developed, every bit of perception Draven had hammered into him in the past six years, that she'd been relieved. It had been in the tone of her voice when she'd said, "Not Daniel?" and in the tiny sigh he'd barely heard when he'd confirmed that.

He'd cautioned her about the source of the information, the tenuousness of the lead, but he knew that had been as much to try to convince himself as her. This lead felt right, and wishing it had been Huntington wouldn't change that.

He caught himself letting the speedometer creep upward far enough past the speed limit to draw any cop's eye. He backed off, wondering how he could be so eager to get to Lilith's and so reluctant at the same time.

He'd told Draven to have Hill stay until he got there, so it wasn't as though he had a choice. Besides, he wanted to do a check of her condo once more, make sure nothing had changed since the last time, and he was the only one who could do that.

Even the thought rang hollow; Lilith was a perceptive, observant woman, and if anything had changed she would notice. Especially now that even she was convinced there was at least some danger to her.

He rubbed his eyes as he drove, suddenly feeling much more tired than even his last few nights of little sleep warranted. Perhaps he should just let the woman handle it, take a break from all this.

But he couldn't. He didn't know Taylor Hill, and while if Draven said she was good, she was good, he didn't *know* that himself.

The realization that hit him then nearly stunned him. He trusted John Draven with his life. Anyone at Redstone would, knowing there was no one better at keeping himself and those in his charge alive and safe. And yet here he was, doubting Draven's faultless judgment in this. Why?

The answer was painfully clear.

Because it was Lilith. And when it came to Lilith, he didn't trust anyone but himself to keep her safe.

"Right," he muttered to himself. "And who's going to keep her safe from you?"

"That," he said aloud into the silence of the car, "is up to you as much as keeping her alive is."

He nearly groaned at the realization he was not only talking to himself but answering himself.

When he pulled into the parking area at the condo, he spotted the car Hill had driven right away, since it was one of the cars from the pool security had access to. It was parked next to

Lilith's dark gray coupe, which had remained in its assigned spot since all this had started.

She'd told him that the other spot was her neighbor's, but since the woman didn't have a car, it wasn't used, and that Mrs. Tilly had offered it to her any time she needed it. It was where he usually parked, but now obviously he'd be relegated to the visitors' section.

Visitor. Yeah, that's what he was, all right. Just a temporary presence in her life, and one she'd like to be rid of as soon as possible, no doubt. As she would be, as soon as this was resolved. She'd go back to her busy, productive, pleasant life, and he'd go back to his busy, productive, empty one, and they'd both think of this as nothing but an interruption in those lives.

Right.

He'd be thinking of this for the rest of that miserable life. Thinking of how close he'd been to the impossible, how he'd had a taste of being with her, only to learn for good that his world, no matter how it had changed, did not blend well with her world.

Because it wasn't really his world that was the problem.

It was him.

He glanced down at the newel posts as he reached the top of the stairs. The grooves from the tightly strung wire were visible, but not glaring.

Kind of like you, he thought wryly. Strung tight but hiding it.

At least, he hoped he was hiding it. From Lilith, anyway.

After he knocked it seemed to take forever for the door to open. He told himself to rein it in, it should take a couple of minutes if Hill was doing her job. And when it did open, it was indeed the new Redstone agent.

Except…she was smiling. Laughing, actually, and it transformed her. No longer was she a plain, ordinary, fade-into-the-background woman. Her eyes fairly sparkled, and for the first time he noticed that they were an unusual shade of hazel flecked with gold. Odd, he thought, he was usually pretty good at details like that.

"Something funny I missed?" he asked as she stood back to let him in.

"No," Hill said. "We were just talking."

"About?" he asked before he could stop himself.

She laughed, and he sensed it was a continuation of the one that had left her face so animated. "Men," she said pointedly.

His mouth twisted wryly. Great. Men, or one man in particular?

As soon as he thought it, he nearly laughed, too. Get over yourself, Alvera. It's not all about you.

He stepped inside and immediately spotted Lilith, who was coming out of the kitchen with a coffee mug in her hand. She, too, was smiling, in a way he hadn't seen since all this had started. As if she, too, had just been laughing and the glee lingered.

He'd never seen her look like that. Even at the Christmas party where he'd first seen her, she'd been restrained, polished...regal had been the word that had come to his mind then.

But then, he told himself as he stood there staring at her, unable to help himself, she'd been two years closer to the hell her ex-husband had put her through. Perhaps that was the answer.

Or perhaps it was just that she and Taylor Hill had hit it off.

Or perhaps, he told himself with an inward grimace, she just doesn't like being around you.

"—asked if you wanted coffee, there's some left."

She was standing in front of him now, a faintly puzzled expression on her face, and he realized she must have already asked him once.

"No."

It sounded abrupt, almost rude, even to his own ears, but it was all he could manage.

"You can leave now, Hill," he said, without looking at the woman.

Lilith blinked. Then she looked at the other woman. "Or you can stay, Taylor. I was enjoying your company."

The implication wasn't lost on Tony, and his jaw tightened.

"You're relieved," he said, more fiercely this time, making sure she realized it was an order, gambling she was too new at the job to want to risk arguing with him. That this was bubbling up out of some silly resentment that Lilith was so relaxed and able to laugh was something he knew on some level, but refused to think about.

To his surprise, Hill stood her ground. "I'd say that's up to Lilith. This is her home."

The two women exchanged a look that made him exceptionally nervous. And made him wonder again exactly what men—or man—they'd been talking about.

"It's all right, Taylor," Lilith said. "We do have some things to discuss."

We do? Tony thought, but said nothing, not wanting anything to delay Hill's quick departure. Why he wanted her gone, and right now, was another thing he didn't want to think about.

Hill hesitated, then nodded. She closed the door quietly behind her as she left.

"Well, that was sufficiently rude."

Stung, he answered before he thought. "What did you expect from somebody like me?"

She drew back slightly. A furrow appeared between her brows as she studied him. The silence spun out long enough to make him uncomfortable, long enough for him to wonder where the hell his professionalism had vanished to.

"I expected," she said finally, "the courtesy anyone from Redstone shows anyone else from Redstone. I expected you to be polite, perhaps even use a little of your famous charm. Not to charge in here and practically throw out a young woman who was only here because you asked her to be."

He felt the jab of guilt because he knew those first and last words were true. But somehow the only thing he could focus on was the other thing she'd said in between.

Famous charm?

He knew it was absurd to get hung up on that amid everything else. But something about the way she had said it was poking at him, and he didn't know why.

It wasn't that he didn't realize what she meant. He'd learned charm at a time when he still wasn't certain he was really going to escape the streets for good. So he hadn't hesitated to use it, justifying it with the excuse that he had to use whatever tools he had if he was going to truly get out.

He had gotten out. And then had come Lisa. And what had happened then had changed everything. Including his use of his *famous charm.*

But Lilith didn't know about Lisa. Even Josh didn't know, not all the details, anyway. No one did, except St. John. And perhaps Draven; St. John might have told him if for no other reason than he'd be thinking maybe Draven should keep an eye on him, see if it was going to affect his work.

But he'd shown them it wouldn't, and now, all these years later, he was sure they'd forgotten all about it.

It was only he who couldn't forget that he'd as good as killed Lisa with his own hands.

Chapter 16

"Sorry to interrupt your little party," Tony muttered, apparently just noticing that there were dishes and Chinese takeout cartons on the coffee table.

"Were we not supposed to eat without your permission?"

Lilith's expression was sweet, her tone deadly. She saw that Tony didn't miss it. But then, it should have been obvious to even the most muddled male mind that he'd crossed a line. And she knew he was very far from stupid, and it didn't take a genius to realize what that line was.

"I am not your ex," he said, seeming to try for a calm, even tone, although he didn't quite achieve it. As if the gruffness had merely been a rough throat, he gave a halfhearted cough. She wondered why he even tried.

"No," Lilith said after a moment. "No, you're not. You were right, you're nothing like him."

"You think I don't know that?"

He was snapping again, as if he couldn't help it. She

could almost see the effort he made as he tried once more to rein it in.

"I'm glad for you," he said.

She wasn't sure what he was talking about, but she knew he didn't mean it. It was so obviously a forced lie that she drew back in puzzlement. "Glad?"

"That it's not him. Obviously that made you…happy."

She stared at him. "Happy?"

"Obviously you still have feelings for him, so of course you'd be relieved it wasn't—"

"Are you out of your mind?"

"Completely," he muttered, so low she wasn't sure she was supposed to have heard it.

"That's a lot of 'obvious' you're throwing around there, and *none* of it is obvious to me. Relieved? Yes, I was relieved. Do you think I want to have to deal with him again, in any way?"

"I—"

"What's wrong?" she asked bluntly, cutting him off. "You've been acting odd ever since the fund-raiser, and you've been behaving worse ever since you got here tonight. Is there something you're not telling me?"

"Yes."

He looked as if he regretted the word the moment it was out.

"What? Tell me."

"Never mind."

"I don't play that game, Tony. Not anymore."

She stood there, toe-to-toe with him, not even close to backing down. It took every bit of the nerve she'd gained in the years since Daniel, to stare down this man who had likely seen and done things that would make her quail.

"You opened this door, you can't slam it again and pretend you never did," she told him, still refusing to back off. "What have you learned? Is it about Chilton?"

"No. Nothing more than you know."

"Then what?"

To her amazement, he looked away, as if he were dodging her. What on earth could make this man, who as a child had faced days when he would see certain cars turn down what had once been a quiet, residential street and had known a hail of bullets was about to start, be afraid to face her?

"I'll have Draven assign Taylor Hill to you," he said, turning away from her now.

"What are you talking about?"

"It will be easier," he said. "She's a woman."

"I noticed."

"You liked her, right?" he said, indicating the dishes and half-empty cartons.

"Yes, I did. She's a bright, very nice young woman."

"So it's no problem, then."

"*What* is no problem?"

She was starting to sound exasperated, while he was desperately trying to avoid saying the one thing he most didn't want to say.

"Having her take over," he finally said.

"Take over?" Comprehension dawned. "You're *quitting?*"

She was astonished; this went against everything she knew of him, of Redstone Security, and of the people Draven selected and trained.

"You're Redstone," she said. "We don't quit."

"I'm not quitting, not really." It sounded like an excuse even he didn't believe. "I'll keep digging, I'll find out what's really going on, I just…can't do this anymore."

Oh, God. Lilith's stomach knotted, and her skin went suddenly clammy and cold.

She had betrayed herself. Somehow. Some way. He knew. She thought she'd successfully hidden her silly, unruly, impossible thoughts about him, but somehow he knew, somehow he'd guessed. And he was trying to extricate himself from a hideously embarrassing situation as gracefully as possible.

She told herself to keep quiet, to just accept and let it be, but she was so mortified she couldn't hold back the words that rose to her lips.

"I've made it impossible for you to go on."

He winced, and she groaned inwardly at her own inability to keep her mouth shut. She turned away then, wishing more than anything that she could run, hide from this, from him. But her days of running and hiding were over.

And then, suddenly, his hands were on her shoulders, turning her back to face him. "It's not you!"

The quick, almost fierce words caught her by surprise.

"It's…me."

She blinked, her gaze drawn unwillingly to his face. His eyes, usually dark, were even darker now, and troubled. On some deep level of her mind she was thinking inanely how exotically beautiful he was, how timeless, how easy it was to picture him in another age, an aristocrat riding the endless miles of his rancho, in charge of all he surveyed.

"I made a mistake, Lilith. I thought I could do this, that I could ignore how I feel enough to do my job."

She went very still. "How you feel?"

"How I've felt," he said, his voice so tight and grim it was more suited to delivering a death notification, "since the first time I saw you."

He released her and turned away, as if unable to meet her eyes after that startling declaration.

Lilith stood there, frozen. To her knowledge, the first time they'd ever met had been at a Redstone Christmas party a couple of years ago. He'd been there to shadow Quinn Rafferty, a high-profile guest of Josh's who had received death threats after the release of his novel, which stepped on some famous toes.

She'd told herself at the time that she remembered him so

vividly because it was unusual for a Redstone Security agent to attend this function in a job capacity; they tended to keep their true function out of view. Lilith guessed that many Redstone people knew members of the security team without realizing it. And perhaps not all of them realized why Tony had been there.

But now she was wondering if perhaps she remembered him so vividly for other reasons entirely.

"I don't understand," she said, knowing it was imperative that she do just that, understand exactly what he'd meant. But she couldn't think of anything else to say, because the only thing it seemed possible he was saying was…well, impossible.

"Of course you don't," Tony said, his back still turned. "Why would you? You're everything I'm not." He laughed, and there wasn't a touch of humor in it. "Maybe that's why I practically fell at your feet."

Lilith's breath caught. "Are you saying—?"

She couldn't finish the question. Tony whipped around then, so quickly she almost took a step back.

"I'm saying I wanted to meet you the minute I saw you in that damned red dress. I wanted to find out all about you. I wanted to know about your work. I wanted to know what you liked, didn't like. I wanted to know who your friends were, and why." His voice broke, went almost unbearably harsh. "I wanted…you."

She stared at him, stunned.

"So," he said, pulling back visibly after that astonishing outpouring, "now you can see why you'll be better off with Hill."

"Past tense."

He went still. "What?"

"You said all that in past tense." She didn't point out the obvious, that if it were truly in the past, there would be no problem now.

His mouth twisted into a wry grimace. "Wishful thinking."

Lilith tried to take a deeper breath, wondering what it was called when you had to remind yourself to do things your body normally did automatically.

But there was nothing normal about this, or her reaction to his words. She didn't know what to feel. Her quick, usually reliable mind seemed to have completely shut down on her. All this time she'd been battling her silly imagination, thinking how humiliated she would be if he had any idea how many times she'd thought of him in a far from professional way, and he hit her with this?

He just stood there, looking at her, as if trying to read her mind from her expression.

"Tony, I'm too old for you," she said, the only thing she could think of when the silence became too much to bear.

"I know you're older than I am."

"Much older."

He frowned. "You can't be *that* much older."

"I met Josh when he was in high school. I was on staff."

That got his attention, as she'd thought it would. "You were really his teacher?"

"I was a teaching assistant. My first year in college. But I could see he was something very special, even at fifteen."

She looked up at him then, smiling almost sadly as she read his expression. "Don't bother with the math. I'll tell you. I'm three years older than Josh. Which makes me, what, fifteen years or so older than you?"

He blinked. "I'm thirty-two."

"Are you?" She'd thought him even younger. Not that it helped much.

"Yes. So it's only twelve years."

"Only?" She managed a laugh that was better than his of moments ago, but not by much.

"When you're on a roll," Tony said, with an odd sort of sternness, "you could run me into the ground. Or Liana, who's almost my age. Nobody at Redstone keeps longer hours than you do, except maybe St. John."

"Thank you. I think. I'm flattered. Really."

"To hell with flattered. I would have preferred interested."

Interested. If you only knew....

"This is..." she said, then stopped, trying to gather her courage. "This is impossible."

"You think I don't know that? Why would you look twice at someone like me when you're used to the Daniel Huntingtons of the world?"

And look where that got me, she thought. "Do you think I'm a fool, Tony?"

He frowned. "You? Hardly. You're one of the smartest people I've ever met."

"Smart doesn't necessarily mean not foolish," she pointed out. "But I would be foolish indeed to fall for the same kind of man twice. I know what that kind of surface charm is worth. Exactly nothing."

He winced, and she realized he was thinking that was at least in part aimed at him.

"I'm not accusing you of that," she said.

"Are you sure?" he said, sounding rueful.

"Yes. I know now you're nothing like him. Daniel's charm masks the fact that there's nothing beneath it. Yours...masks that there's too much."

He drew back slightly, his dark eyes widening as if in shock. "Lilith..."

"Josh rarely makes mistakes about people," she said. "And if I forgot that for a while with you, it was because of the unpleasant shock of having my ex-husband shoved back into my world. I reacted as I once did, defensively against any man. I'm sorry about that."

The shock she'd seen gave way to something else, something she couldn't quite name, as he stared down at her. The only word she could put to it was pride, but that made no sense at all.

"You are...amazing," he said softly.

To her astonishment, she felt her cheeks heat. She rarely blushed; it happened only when her emotions were running too high to control.

Like now.

"Does that mean if it weren't for those twelve years, you'd be...?"

"Interested?" She nearly laughed out loud again. But somehow she couldn't bring herself to lie about it. "Oh, yes. I'd be interested. You're fairly amazing yourself, Mr. Alvera."

The look he gave her then was one of such heat that she nearly recoiled from it.

"Good," he said. Sharply. Succinctly.

And Lilith suddenly realized she'd made a serious miscalculation. She'd thought she was firmly closing a door that should never be opened.

She hadn't taken into account that Tony Alvera was not the kind of man to let a mere closed—or even locked—door stop him.

Chapter 17

He went over her condo inch by inch but found nothing. No sign that anyone had tried any windows, no new marks on the doors or the locks.

He still didn't like that damned balcony, not when anyone with decent balance and a bit of strength could get to it from the landscaping wall below, or even more easily from the neighbor's balcony.

Out on the landing he checked the front door and its serviceable dead bolt once more. Then, as if there were some clue there he'd missed, he crouched down again to look at the grooves in the wood newel posts.

His thought about the neighbor's balcony coming back to him, he took a look at the door at the other end of the landing. Lilith had told him Mrs. Tilly was like a one-woman neighborhood watch; she had a lot of spare time and didn't miss much. Except when she got on the phone with her daughter in Arizona,

Lilith told him; then the world could cave in and she wouldn't pay any attention.

An old lady like that might seem like a tempting pathway to her neighbor, he thought. It wouldn't take much to break in, overpower her and simply wait on that balcony for Lilith to arrive home.

But there was no sign of tampering there, either—although he would ask to inspect the inside, later, to be sure—and he went back to those infuriating grooves in the wood again.

Apparently the neighborhood watch aspect was in full force, because it wasn't long before Mrs. Tilly opened her door and stepped out onto the landing.

"Lilith told me it wasn't the Wells boy after all," the woman said without preamble. "Is that true? I thought she was just being soft. Why, she's even thinking about getting the boy's mother a job at that Redstone place."

"No, I don't think it was him," he said, thinking again how like Lilith that would be. "But it was someone."

"Is what happened why you've been coming here with Lilith all the time?"

Whether she fell into the nosy or concerned category, he wasn't sure. Lilith said concerned, but then she was a generous soul.

He gave himself a mental tug when he felt himself start to veer down the road of all the other things Lilith was. "What makes you think that? Maybe I'm…a new boyfriend."

Mrs. Tilly snorted incredulously. Tony tried not to be insulted. When the woman went on, it was easier as it became clear what she'd meant.

"Lilith? That girl barely takes time to breathe. Told her for years she needs a man in her life, but she just laughs and says work is safer."

Safer.

The word made him wince inwardly. A memory of his mother, crying in the rocking chair that had been her mother's in turn, because she no longer felt safe in her home, burned through his mind. But at least that threat had been from outside.

He couldn't imagine how it must feel to have the threat come from inside, and from the very person whose main concern should be keeping you safe.

So now that's your concern, he told himself. Get to it.

When the woman had gone back inside—and quickly secured her dead bolt lock—Tony continued downstairs and headed for his car. Lilith was safely inside now; he could think. He would call Hill, have her come back, then…

Then what?

He had no idea.

He yanked the driver's door closed with more energy than was necessary, and the slam settled his nerves a bit. He *did* need to focus on this. Anything else—if there was anything else—would simply have to wait.

It was dark enough now that the automatic sensors turned on the headlights. He drove slowly down the row of covered parking stalls. He didn't like the things, didn't like the vehicles being outside and vulnerable. Most people didn't, he supposed, but their concerns were usually limited to weathering and the occasional vandalism.

He tried not to glance over at Lilith's car, at the now empty parking spot beside it. Ridiculously, his hands tightened on the wheel, and he realized he was fighting the urge to turn in and park there.

And do what? he asked himself. Go back up, confront her, start one of Those Conversations any man in his right mind tried his damnedest to avoid?

She'd already made it pretty clear how she felt. She thought she was too old for him.

Or maybe that you're too young for her, he amended silently, finally giving in and glancing at that tempting empty space as he went slowly past.

He hit the brakes sharply.

For an instant he just stared, wondering if he was imagining things because he'd just been thinking of the hazards of unsecured parking. But he knew it was there, that gleaming bit of fluid creeping out from under Lilith's car, reflecting the headlight's glare.

He was out in an instant, the flashlight from his glove compartment in hand, kneeling beside the drying puddle. In the fading light it was difficult to tell, but it didn't look like the greenish color of coolant, or the red of transmission or steering fluid, not even the darker shade of engine oil. It looked almost clear, just faintly golden.

Suspicion bit deep, and he reached down to touch the wettest part of the small seepage. He rubbed the liquid between his fingers.

Not just wet. Not oily. Slippery.

Very slippery.

Brake fluid.

He was on his back and under the car in seconds. He traced the brake line with the beam of light. He found no visible drip, but after a moment spotted a point on the line that looked cleaner than the rest. He touched it, and his fingertip came away once more slick and slippery. He focused the flashlight there, saw a barely perceptible puncture. Slightly elongated, as if it could have been made with the tip of a pocketknife, just enough to cause a very slow leak.

He swore viciously under his breath, wondering how he could have missed this. That Hill had apparently missed it as well registered, and he thought it was a good thing the woman was gone or he might have chewed a piece off her, and that was Draven's job.

The puddle was dry enough that it likely had been there awhile. It was just barely visible beyond the edge of her car's shadow, and they hadn't really gone near her car all week, but that, to him, was no excuse.

Not when it was Lilith.

Not when this might well have succeeded in killing her. They obviously had every reason to think she'd have continued to drive this car, and the results eventually could have been disastrous.

The thought chilled him much more than the cool asphalt at his back.

It was time to get his freaking head back in the game.

Chapter 18

She opened the door hesitantly.

"I'd ask if you forgot something, but I know you didn't," she said.

Just my mind, he thought as he stared at her. She'd changed into some bluish-looking outfit, loose pants and a sweatshirt-type top, but it was in a fuzzy material he just knew would feel like warm velvet. The sheen of it seemed to ripple over her, changing with her every move, every breath. Her hair was pulled back into a tail at her nape, and he thought for all her concern about being older than he, at the moment she looked about twenty.

He stepped inside, pushing past her, unable to resist the slightest brush of his fingers over that fabric; it felt even better than he'd imagined.

And she felt more tempting beneath it than anything he could ever remember.

"Put some clothes on," he said, hating the snap that had come into his voice. "We're getting out of here."

"I believe I have clothes on," she said mildly.

Put something on that won't drive me insane, he amended, then held his breath, half-afraid he'd said it out loud. When she just continued to look at him with that cool, assessing expression, he pulled his thoughts together.

With an effort, he presented her with a concise report of what he'd found. Then he got back to his original order.

"Get what you need, while I figure out where we're going."

"I am not leaving home," Lilith said firmly.

"That wasn't a request," Tony retorted.

"You said yourself it probably happened some time ago," she pointed out with annoying reasonability. "The spot was nearly dry, you said."

"Never mind what I said. It's still twice they've come after you here."

"Maybe, but couldn't it just as easily have been the same time? The brakes as backup in case the wire didn't work? I haven't driven the car since that day, and you said it was a small leak."

"Stop repeating what I said," he snapped.

He knew she was right, but he didn't want to admit it now that it was helping her avoid doing what he wanted her to do.

"So there's no reason to assume the threat has suddenly become more...immediate," she said. The fact that she wasn't denying that there indeed was a threat mollified him a little. But not much.

"Reason," he muttered, "doesn't seem to have much to do with it."

"What?"

"Nothing. You can't stay here."

She smothered a sigh. "You're not listening."

"I heard you."

"Tony—"

"You want to die to prove me right?"

The sharpness of his tone got through to her. But she didn't buckle. He wondered—if her life had been different, if she hadn't had to learn to stand up to her ex, would she have given in by now? Ironic that, without even trying, Daniel Huntington was still affecting her.

"I'm through running," she said. "There has to be another way. If you must, have Taylor come back."

He took a breath, amazed that it took conscious effort. "No. If you won't go, I'm staying."

Lilith simply looked at him, as if she were pondering the ramifications of his decision—one that he hadn't even realized he'd made until this moment—not to call back the other agent.

Whatever her thoughts were, they didn't show. But then, she'd likely had a lot of practice hiding her thoughts from her ex-husband. That she would use that skill with him rankled, but he supposed she felt she had to. Now that he'd blurted out his idiot attraction to her.

He thought she was going to argue with him, insist that he leave, that she'd be fine here alone.

"I'm staying," he said again. "Damned if I'm going to face Josh and have to tell him I let something happen to someone who matters to him as much as you do. So I'm staying. Whether it's in here or out in my car is up to you."

There. He'd put it nicely in the context of it being his job. And bringing Josh back into it had been a master stroke, he told himself. She couldn't—wouldn't—argue with that. Nobody from Redstone would.

And she didn't.

"There's a lot of Chinese left," was all she said. "You might as well eat, then."

He blinked. "What?"

"I'll warm it up."

She was merely being polite, he knew; she had the leftover food, so he might as well eat it. There was nothing about her capitulation or her manner to indicate they were going to head into any deep, emotional discussion of his unwise confession.

And what about hers?

Oh, yes. I'd be interested. You're fairly amazing yourself, Mr. Alvera.

Her words echoed in his head, replaying in an audio loop that seemed endless. The part of him that wanted to seize on those words and go after what they implied was warring with the part of him that told him this was a job, and he needed to focus on that until he was sure she was safe. She was Redstone, and therefore his responsibility. She was one of Josh's oldest and dearest friends, which made that even more imperative. He'd told the truth about that.

When he'd finished the meal, or at least as much as he'd been able to force down, he sat at the cool granite bar in her kitchen, poking the last grains of rice around with the fork she'd given him when he'd told her chopsticks weren't part of his milieu. He knew he had yet another battle in front of him, and he didn't even know how to start.

"I have some work to do," she said as she opened the dishwasher and put in the plates she and Taylor had used. He set down the fork and picked up both it and the plate he'd used, then walked around the end of the dining bar to add them to the collection in the rack.

At her glance, he shrugged. "I'm housebroken. My mother never had a dishwasher when I was at home, but she made sure Lucy and I cleaned up after ourselves."

"Lucy?"

"Lucinda. My sister." He got it out evenly enough. "My mother cleaned up after my father. It was their way."

"I didn't realize you had a sister. Where is she now?"

"Dead," he said shortly, wishing he'd never let the name slip out. Something about this woman made him lose his usual care about speaking without thinking. He'd never really been aware how much of a buffer that studied flattery, the surface flirting created between him and every woman he dealt with, until he'd stopped using it on her. It hadn't even been a conscious decision, it just hadn't seemed right. Those practiced words and gestures were for casual acquaintances, for friends who didn't mind the teasing nature of it, and for those he needed to finagle something from. Lilith wasn't any of those.

He just wasn't sure what she was.

"I'm sorry, Tony."

Her words were soft, and the long, silent moment she'd waited before saying them somehow took them out of the realm of automatic platitude.

"It was a long time ago." He was sounding gruff again, but he couldn't help that.

"She must have been very young, then."

"Fifteen."

"That's horrible," she said. "Was she ill?"

He blinked. Then laughed harshly. "Of course you'd assume that. In your world, if a fifteen-year-old dies, it's illness, or maybe an accident. In mine, the first possibility that comes to anyone's mind is a drive-by bullet."

To her credit, although she paled, she didn't back away. "Is that what happened?"

"She wasn't even out on the street. She was in her bedroom, trying on her new dress for her fifteenth birthday. We buried her in it, instead."

"I am sorry, Tony. There's no excuse for that."

"They paid," he said succinctly. He waited for her to ask, realized he was angry, wanted her to say something silly about the law and vengeance so he could unload all his tangled emotions. But instead she simply nodded, a little sharply, and said just one word.

"Good."

She left him there, staring after her, as she went into the den that she used as an office. For a moment he couldn't move. He so rarely talked about Lucy, he was a little stunned that it had come out so easily.

Only one secret left, *vato,* he told himself.

Since it was the one most likely to actually send her running, he didn't know if he would ever spill it.

Finally he walked to the door of her office, watching as she waited for the desktop computer to finish booting, then picked up the small flash drive that sat beside the keyboard and plugged it in.

"You don't get enough of this ten, twelve hours a day at Redstone?" he asked.

"Josh brought me in to clean up this mess, and until we're sure we've found everything that Stan Chilton might have tampered with or sold, then no, I haven't done enough."

"Josh wouldn't expect you to drive yourself into the ground."

"Yet he would, for me. Or anyone else Redstone."

Tony couldn't argue with that. And since he had another unpleasant surprise for her later, he left her in peace for the moment. He couldn't help her with what she was doing, apparently searching some huge database that had been on that little USB drive; he was competent enough using a computer, but this kind of process was out of his league. She'd probably laugh at him if she knew he sometimes resorted to plain old pen and paper, with a small notebook he carried in a jacket pocket, but sometimes he felt better being able to be sure sensitive information had been destroyed. A computer file seemed to exist in some form forever.

He went back into the living room, sat down on the couch where she and Hill had been sharing dinner and that talk about men, or whatever it was that had had them laughing. He couldn't relax and was soon back on his feet, wandering around the room, checking windows he'd already checked and the front door he'd already made certain was securely dead-bolted.

He paused as he passed a large bookshelf at one end of the room. It was full, not just with several shelves of books—mysteries, biographies and, he noted with a bemused inward smile, apparently the entire *Harry Potter* series—but a shelf of DVDs in a similar vein. CDs took up another shelf, everything from country to alternative rock to Beethoven. Eclectic, he thought, wasn't the word for it. There was much more to Lilith Mercer than that polished exterior might suggest.

He barely stopped himself from making another tour of the condo, checking all the doors and windows yet again. The only thing that allowed him to rein in the urge was the fact that she was trying to work. Instead he paced the living room, trying to halt his careening mind instead. Here he was, at home with the woman who'd captured his imagination so thoroughly that he'd never forgotten her even though, before Beck's case had come up, he'd barely ever seen her. And he couldn't do a damn thing about it. He was here to protect her, keep her safe.

And that included from him.

Almost desperately he picked up a book at random; he would have chosen the TV, but didn't want to disturb her work. He sat down in the chair closest to the window that looked out on the front landing; he didn't expect a repeat of the wire trick, but he also didn't take anything for granted. There was an ottoman next to it, and he stretched his legs out and settled in; he didn't know how long she planned on working, only that she never seemed to stop.

He started to read, but found himself having to go back and reread a section every few pages. The more he thought about what Lilith had said, the more he thought she was probably right; the brakes and the wire had been rigged at the same time. He had no idea if the cut in the brake line had been purposely small, making for a slow leak that would gradually drain the system, or if the culprit had just been in a hurry. Either way, it was sloppy if the intent was murder.

Then again, so was the wire. True, a tumble down the full flight of concrete steps could have proved fatal, but just as likely, had her reflexes not been so good, Lilith could have been just badly injured.

He cringed inwardly at the thought of her broken from such a fall, or from some horrible crash when her brakes finally gave out at just the wrong moment….

So was that the goal? he wondered. Was it to injure rather than kill? And if so, why? If it had been her ex, he could have understood it; that kind of emotional involvement sometimes required inflicting lasting pain, and shied away from the death that would also mean the absence of someone to hate. He'd seen it before, people who were so focused on the object of their hatred that once it was removed, when they by rights should have been happy, they instead lost their driving force and drifted, rudderless, unsure what to do with themselves now that the hate that had defined them for so long had no object.

But Stan Chilton didn't even know Lilith, from all he could determine. There was nothing personal involved; she was nothing more to him than the person brought in to clean up his mess. So why not just kill her outright?

Except that that wasn't logical, either. As Draven had said, it was he and Ian and Samantha Gamble who had brought Chilton down. Chilton should be after them.

So why Lilith? It made no sense to him.

Which was, he admitted, probably the problem; looking for logic in screwed up minds like Chilton's was a mistake to begin with. If the man had been merely after money—although with what Redstone paid that was hard to believe—it would have been cut-and-dried. But he'd been nursing a fierce case of envy—envy of Ian's brilliance and success under the Redstone wing—and that had contorted his existing sense of entitlement into something twisted and evil.

He grimaced, both at the tangled mess this was, and at the

irony that it made street gang violence seem simple. Ugly, yes, but simple; you hit us, we hit back, harder. Stray onto our turf at your own risk. Black and white, it was what it was.

"Problem?"

Jerked back to the present by her quiet query, Tony gave up any pretense of reading and slammed the book closed; even magic wasn't enough of a distraction at the moment. He sat upright, surprised at how long he'd been sitting here unraveling; it was full dark now. A glance at his watch told him it was nearly ten.

"Same old," he muttered. He didn't explain whether it was her situation or just her, and she thankfully didn't press him.

She sat down on the edge of the ottoman his feet had just vacated. Close. Too close. "I can't make any sense out of it, either."

That her words could apply to either thing he'd been wrestling with didn't escape him, but he took the more prudent route. Especially with her sitting so damned close.

"Somebody told me once that every mind, even a sick one, works out its own logic," he said.

She pondered that for a moment. "Draven?" she guessed.

He shook his head. "Actually, St. John."

Her brows rose. "The mystery man?"

It was an appellation applied frequently to Josh's enigmatic right-hand man, the man rarely seen by anyone outside—some speculated because he never left his penthouse apartment on the top floor of Redstone Headquarters—and not all that often by Redstone people themselves.

"I don't know what his life has been, but I have a feeling it just might make mine look tame."

"Hard to believe," Lilith said.

"I don't have the corner on dubious pasts."

She gave him an odd little smile he couldn't quite interpret. "Funny, I never thought of your past as dubious. Heartrending, yes, and painful, but not dubious."

He swallowed against the sudden tightness in his throat. He'd long ago gotten over the fact that almost everyone at Redstone knew where he'd come from, just as they knew the story of how he'd been given a way out by Josh. But until now, he hadn't really considered the logical fact that some had actually spent time thinking about it.

That one of them had apparently been Lilith unsettled him.

He barely managed not to leap up just to put some more space between them. He could smell her, that rich, luscious scent he'd come to associate with her. He'd seen a bottle of perfume in her bathroom, something gardenia, so he supposed that's what it was. Whatever the name, it was driving him crazy, and he knew that whenever he smelled anything like it, he was forever going to think of her.

"Doing a pretty good job of that now," he muttered to himself.

"I'm going to bed," she said.

At least he'd armored himself for that one. Not that the simple words didn't conjure up a host of vivid images he could have done without. Or at least, could have done without just now; if he were alone, he wouldn't mind dwelling on each one in turn at length.

"Fine. Move what you need in there." He gestured toward the second bedroom.

She took a step back, her eyes widening. "I beg your pardon?"

So polite, he thought. Always so polite. "You're not sleeping in that bedroom with the balcony."

She stared at him as if the only thing she could think of to say was what she had just said, so she wasn't going to say anything. But he also saw her delicate jaw set, and knew he was going to have a fight on his hands. He wasn't in the mood.

So instead of trying to persuade her with convincing arguments, he cut straight to the one he figured would win the quickest.

"You have two options," he said evenly. "First, you sleep in the guest room without the balcony."

She arched a brow at him. "Or?"

"Or you sleep in your bedroom, in your bed...with me."

He watched the color flood her cheeks. Watched her lips part as if she were having trouble taking a breath.

And he held his own, trying not to admit to the simple fact that, no matter how insane, no matter how impossible, he wanted more than anything for her to choose the second option.

Chapter 19

There were women she knew, Lilith thought, who could take such a statement and handle it coolly, with a blasé sort of acceptance—of course men made offers such as this, it was their due—that she'd always admired but never been able to perfect herself.

Then again, she doubted any of them had ever had an offer—or ultimatum—like this given to them by a man like Antonio Diego Alvera Bernard.

She wondered if any woman he really set his sights on had ever, could ever, refuse him.

She wondered if, had he been serious instead of obviously trying to goad her into doing what he wanted for her own safety, she could have refused him.

But it was clear that was what he was doing. Despite his earlier, surprising confession, she knew that he was simply using this to provoke her into doing what he thought best.

It was, she thought, a form of manipulation. He'd said it just to get her to recoil and do as she was told. He couldn't really—

"Don't," he said, his voice no longer provoking but quiet, almost imploring, all challenge gone, vanished. "Whatever you're thinking, whatever you're telling yourself, don't. I meant what I said."

Her breath caught in her throat and it was a moment before she regained enough of it to speak. All of her umbrage at the transparent manipulation vanished. If he'd meant it…

"Tony, you can't—"

"Don't tell me what I can't think, or feel, or want. And you don't have to tell me you're out of my league, I know that."

"I don't believe in that tripe, and I would never say such—"

"I know you wouldn't. You don't have to say it, it's obvious. But I just tonight realized that even though I know it, I don't care."

She stared at him, seeing something in his dark eyes that she'd never seen before, never thought to see, not in this man. Not a softness, that word could never apply to him, but just a hint of vulnerability, as if she had some sort of power over him. And that he was expecting her to use it.

Realization flooded her. He did mean what he'd said. All of it. Including that he thought her out of his league, as he'd put it. She tilted her head slightly as she explored the revelation that had struck her.

"After I left Daniel," she said slowly, "it was weeks before I stopped jumping at any sound behind me."

He grimaced, and she held up a hand before he could say the terse opinion of her ex-husband she sensed was on the tip of his tongue.

"It took longer for me to be able to view the approach of any man without suspicion. And longer still before I could make the change from expecting the worst to assuming others meant me no harm."

"I would never hurt you."

She doubted that, although she knew he never would in the way he meant it, physically, as Daniel had hurt her. Emotionally, she wasn't so sure. But she also wasn't sure whose fault that would be, if she were to be so foolish as to give free rein to tangled emotions.

"I know that. Because I've left that past behind. It shaped me, yes. But it doesn't rule me." She looked at him steadily. "Can you say that?"

He blinked. Drew back slightly. "What?"

"Aren't you letting your past rule you? You've come so far from those mean streets, and yet they're never that far away in your mind."

"I don't want to forget where I came from."

"Of course you don't. Nor should you. You should be proud that you survived, prouder yet that you got out. It can't have been easy, even with Josh's help."

"Then your point?" He said it stiffly, as if she'd offended him somehow. But she slogged on, anyway.

"Do you really want to live like you're still there?"

He stood up then. Instinctively she rose as well, unwilling to let him tower over her. This was important, she sensed, or he wouldn't be reacting like this.

"You say I'm out of your league," she repeated quietly, "but the only one keeping you in the league you think you're in, is you."

He stared down at her. She stood her ground. It was a hard-learned lesson that took hard-won nerve, but she didn't, couldn't falter, not now, not here, not with this man at this time.

The hush spun out so long she didn't know if she could stand it. She'd never been one who felt she had to fill any silent moment with chatter, but this was different. She couldn't help imagining that if only her hearing were a tiny bit more acute, she'd be able to hear the crackle of electricity between them.

Finally, in a voice that sounded strung almost as tight as the tension in the room, he said, "Are you choosing option B?"

She opened her mouth to say "Of course not!" But the words

didn't come. Because she wasn't sure it was true. Had she, on some level, been saying yes?

For a moment, just a moment, her heart jumped to her throat, her pulse began to hammer, and an odd combination of heat and chill gripped her.

But then reality flooded back, taking with it the urge to leap that she'd been so close to.

"I…I'm flattered, really," she said, hating the sound of the words even as she said them. But the cold truth still remained. "But I'm still old enough to be your…aunt," she finished lamely, falling back on the old analogy she'd been clinging to since the day she realized this man was going to be in her pocket for the foreseeable future.

"I have three aunts, all of them are years older than you and I don't need or want another."

His voice was harsh, and she suddenly realized he'd put his hands on her shoulders. Gently, with none of the bruising grip Daniel had used, but still firmly. She had the oddest feeling that if he weren't doing that, his hands might be shaking. That image, of this man, so tough, so strong, sent ripples of that chilling heat through her all over again.

"We're going to continue this discussion," he said, his voice barely above a whisper now, "but first…"

She knew before he moved what he was going to do. Common sense told her to stop him before he started, but the combination of that rising heat, the tingling of every nerve and the lack of air to breathe drowned out her own warning.

When his mouth came down on hers she nearly gasped at the sweet shock of it. It felt as if she'd been waiting for this for years. It wasn't that she hadn't been kissed since Daniel; she had. But never by anyone she'd wanted it from more, and that was a fact she only now admitted, even to herself.

She had thought she might never truly trust a man again. She had accepted that possibility and gone on, thinking that if she ever came across a man who could accept that limitation, she might even venture into a relationship of sorts, the best she could hope for under the circumstances. And there had been a couple of men who had been willing to try, but in the end had given up, unable to stick it out for the length of time it had taken her to get around to trusting them.

But she trusted this man. Maybe it was because he was Redstone, maybe it was because Josh had trusted him first and he was so rarely wrong. But whatever the reason, in this case the trust had come first. Perhaps that was why, in this moment, all the feelings she'd kept banked and under wraps for so long burst free at the first touch of his lips on hers, heedless of all the reasons why this was probably the least wise thing she could ever do.

And then thought fled, burned away at the testing flick of his tongue over her lower lip. She heard an odd little moan, realized it had come from her and almost pulled away. As if he'd sensed her retreat, he pulled her closer, deepening the kiss, giving her more of the hot, incredible sensation. Things seemed to spin around her, and she wondered if he truly had somehow sucked all the air out of room.

When he finally broke away, she nearly let out that moan again, at the loss of his heat, his touch, his taste. When he let go of her shoulders, she thought she might fall. She was almost afraid to open her eyes, afraid to see what would be in his face, afraid to look up and see the Tony Alvera she'd seen in action, the incurable flirt his reputation held he was, afraid she'd see some kind of smug satisfaction in those dark eyes, as if he'd proven she was as susceptible to his charms as any woman.

But she did; she'd long ago quit avoiding the things she was most afraid of, another hard-learned lesson.

He was staring at her, that much was true to her imagining. But she could never have envisioned the look of wonder that she saw now on his face; she wouldn't even have begun to guess he could look that way.

She wasn't ready for this. She wasn't even sure what it was, this fierce, hot feeling. But that she was even experiencing it at all, in terms that hinted that at some point she might be ready, shocked her.

She saw him swallow as if his throat was as tight as her own.

"Aunt?" he whispered. "I think not."

Tony stared at the closed bathroom door. She'd retreated to her bedroom as if it were some sort of sanctuary, then to the bathroom to do whatever it was women did to get ready for sleep.

He'd have thought she was running from him, if he hadn't known she never ran from anything.

Sleep was the only thing that was on the agenda tonight, he knew. He'd expected no less. He'd already gotten more than he ever expected, in the way she'd responded to him, the way she'd gone soft and warm, the way she'd kissed him back.

And even if it never went beyond that kiss, he'd carry the sound of that tiny moan she'd made to his grave.

But it was that tiny moan that also gave him hope, hope that maybe, just maybe, she wasn't quite as far out of reach as he'd thought.

...the only one keeping you in the league you think you're in, is you.

Her words came back to him as he stood in the doorway of the bedroom he still wasn't going to let her sleep in. Was she right? Did he truly carry his past around with him like some baggage loaded with graffitied bricks? Had this woman, who had a different but just as heavy a load of memories to carry, in fact done a better job than he had of getting past them?

You should be proud that you survived, prouder yet that you got out.

He was proud, he thought. He'd never taken Josh's generosity for granted. He'd worked hard, he'd been determined, had fought for this chance, knowing full well it would likely be the only one he ever got. He'd just never thought it had earned him the right to move in her kind of world.

But was he wrong? Was it possible that it didn't really matter, at least to her?

He flicked a glance at that closed bathroom door, trying not to let his mind careen down the dangerous path of wondering what she wore to bed. Some elegant, lacy thing? Some swath of shimmering satin that would glide over her like that damned red dress he'd never been able to get out of his head? Or, aware of his presence, would she instead armor herself in something heavy and concealing? Not that it would matter; after that dress he was too well able to imagine the body beneath for camouflage to have much effect.

He made himself turn his gaze to the sliding glass doors that led to that damned balcony. He was tempted to go over and open it, leave it open not for the cool breeze but as an irresistible temptation to whoever was after her. If she wasn't here, he would do it.

Grateful for the distraction as he waited for her to finish, he turned the idea over in his mind. He could enlist Mrs. Tilly; she clearly liked Lilith and would likely help. And Hill, although she probably wouldn't be thrilled to work with him after he'd summarily dismissed her tonight. But she was Redstone, and she'd help, no matter what.

He'd send Mrs. Tilly off to visit her daughter for a few days, he thought, courtesy of Redstone. Few people could resist a free trip, especially when it was on one of the Redstone fleet of Hawk jets. He knew that if he said it was necessary, Redstone would foot the bill for the whole trip without a question; it was part of the extreme trust Josh had in his people.

That would give him a base to work from. Lilith could come home with Hill, as she had tonight, he thought. He would be next door, and would help Lilith make the too-easy climb from her own balcony to Mrs. Tilly's. And then Hill could make a show of leaving, waving and talking as if Lilith were still inside, indicating she was now home alone.

It might take a couple of days, but sooner or later that fish was going to bite. And he'd be waiting. He could take up a position here, or just stay on Mrs. Tilly's balcony and wait.

He was still considering all the possible facets to this plan when he heard the door open. He braced himself, then turned his head.

No lacy, sheer thing. No sweep of red satin. Not even the flannel-type armor he'd imagined.

Lilith Mercer, high-class, elegant, polished Lilith Mercer apparently slept in a hockey jersey.

He nearly laughed at the incongruity of it. Would have, if it hadn't bared so much of those long, luscious legs he'd imagined so often. Would have, if he hadn't been able to tell, when she moved, that her breasts were free beneath the slippery fabric.

Would have, if it hadn't made her look so tiny, almost fragile.

A sudden image of Daniel Huntington snapped into his mind. The man was as big as he was, and the idea of Huntington hitting this woman, of him using a crude, brutal weapon on her, striking what could so easily have been a fatal blow, made a protective urge that dwarfed everything he'd felt before nearly swamp him.

No matter what it took, he would keep this woman safe. He couldn't let himself be distracted from that task. Not by anything. And if that meant he had to keep his own feelings on a tight leash, so be it. He'd done harder things.

Maybe.

Chapter 20

When the phone rang at three in the morning, it didn't wake Tony. He was already awake. Had been, most of the night. It had nothing to do with the sofa in the living room he was lying on—it was actually comfortable—and everything to do with the visions of the woman sleeping just down the hall that he couldn't seem to get out of his head.

But when the phone stopped abruptly in the middle of the third ring, a different image of her suddenly flashed through his mind, the image of her picking up the cordless phone from her nightstand in the master bedroom and taking it with her to the guest room.

He hadn't said anything; she wasn't arguing with him about sleeping in the other room, so he'd decided to leave well enough alone. Whether she just couldn't bear to be out of touch, or whether she got late night calls from someone he didn't know about, was something that was going to have to wait.

But 3:00 a.m. didn't qualify as simply late night.

He was on his feet, kicking aside the blanket she'd given him. In seconds he was at the door of the guest room. He paused for a moment, listening, but heard no sound of voices through the closed door. There was, he'd noted earlier, no lock, as there was on the master, so he hadn't had to bring up the possibly touchy subject of her locking it or not.

He gave a courtesy tap on the door but didn't wait to open it.

The room was dark, but his eyes were adjusted; he hadn't been foolish enough to turn on a light and destroy that. She sat up in the double bed that was the lower bunk of the childishly decorated room, looking sleepy and puzzled. He could see that the phone receiver sat quietly on the bedside table. If he hadn't been certain, he might have thought he'd imagined the ring.

And then her expression changed, and she pulled the covers closer around her, as if they were that armor she'd not put on. And he realized she was wondering exactly why he was in her doorway.

In her room, he corrected himself silently, only now realizing he'd taken a couple of strides past the door.

"Who was it?" he said.

She moved then, reaching up to click on the bedside lamp. He instantly missed the intimacy of the darkness, then wondered if that was exactly why she'd done it.

She squinted against the flare of light, looking up at him. "No one."

"Lilith, I can't do my job if you—"

"It was a hang-up call," she said with an air of strained patience.

He didn't like that answer, either. "Were you planning to tell me about it?"

She lifted a brow at him. "At a decent hour in the morning, yes. Wake you up to tell you at 3:00 a.m.? No."

"I was awake."

"I'm sorry it woke you."

"I was already awake," he amended.

"I offered you the other bed," she pointed out.

She had. If she was going to sleep in here at his order, he then was welcome to her bed, she'd said. The only conditions under which he'd make it to her bed, he was sure.

Fortunately for his sanity, his newly discovered masochistic streak hadn't run to subjecting himself to a night in her bed without her. He could only imagine what it would be like to slip between those sheets that likely smelled of that damned gardenia stuff. His dreams were out of control enough already.

He looked at her now, sitting there in that jersey, looking a world removed from the woman she was during the day. Whatever she'd felt when he'd kissed her, she was obviously over it now.

Which fit neatly into his new resolve to keep this hunger he had for her on its chain.

"It's not the couch," he said. "It's fine."

He stopped himself from adding, "It's you." That wouldn't fit at all into his new resolve.

He yanked himself back to business. "They said nothing? At all?"

"No. Not a word."

"Could you hear anything?"

"I could tell it was an open line, that's all. No background noise if that's what you mean."

"Breathing?"

"No. Heavy or otherwise."

If it was an attempt at a joke, he didn't smile. But neither did she, so perhaps she was merely reporting.

"Caller ID?"

"Restricted number," she said. He frowned. She picked up the phone and held it out to him. "Check for yourself."

He believed her, but he took the phone anyway. When he didn't even glance at it she gave him a questioning look.

"The next middle-of-the-night caller is going to get me, not you," he said.

He half expected a fight over this, too, but she merely shrugged. "Fine. But if you decide to answer it in daylight, let me know first. The shock might kill my mother when she calls."

He blinked. That *had* to have been a joke. Didn't it? He couldn't seem to stop himself from asking, "Would the idea of a man answering her daughter's phone really be such a shock to her?"

"It would."

He studied her for a long, silent moment. Then, against every bit of his better judgment, he asked softly, "Have you been…with anyone since your ex?" He saw her go still.

"Are you asking that professionally or personally?"

"Whichever will get me an answer."

"Is that how it works? That charm of yours? If you can't get the answer asking honestly, you make it seem personal and hope no woman can resist?"

He frowned again. This frontal, almost snappish attack wasn't her usual approach. It occurred to him to wonder if it was his question, or simply the setting, being alone with him in a bedroom, while he was fully dressed and all she had on was that silly jersey with the big 66 on it, that had her on edge.

"I still need that answer," he said, ignoring her dig. "Make it a professional inquiry if you want. Because it is that as well. If there's somebody else in this mix, like a disgruntled ex-boyfriend, I need to know."

"How convenient," she muttered.

"Lilith," he began, but stopped when she held up a hand as if she were too weary to argue with him.

"No," she said. "There's no one. Beyond a lunch now and then, or a date for an official function, there hasn't been. Satisfied as to the pitiful state of my social life?"

I was more concerned about your love life, he thought.

Did the two even intersect, in her world? Or did women there keep a very presentable man like Daniel Huntington around for show, and then turn elsewhere for sex? He couldn't imagine

Lilith doing that, but some of the others he'd seen at that fund-raiser? Absolutely.

Hell, maybe he was wrong about all of them. Maybe Lilith was right, and even his perceptions were weighed down by all that street-level baggage he seemed to be lugging around.

And maybe all his thoughts were clouded by the gut-level realization that even if Lilith were like that, he'd want to be the one she turned to for sex. Even if she would never be seen with him in public.

It was going to be, Lilith thought, a very long weekend at this rate.

After that 3:00 a.m. interruption—and the unsettling conversation with Tony Alvera—she hadn't gone back to sleep until nearly five. She'd then slept until just after eight, and still felt groggy.

At least, she had until now, but Tony's calm announcement that he was glued to her hip for the remainder of the weekend shocked her out of the fog and left her gaping.

"I have plans," she snapped. "Not everything requires a man around, you know."

"Fine," he said, unruffled. "Continue with them. I'll drive."

"I'm going shopping," she threatened, although she'd had no such plan.

"I'll carry bags."

She thought of adding "for lingerie," in the hopes of embarrassing him, as it would many men, but she had the sinking suspicion he'd just grin at her and give her an enthusiastic "Good!" Instead she went for the worst female cliché she could think of, even though it was one she'd never been prone to.

"Shoes," she said. "I'll be trying on dozens of shoes."

"I'll wait."

Lord, the perfect man, she thought. For many women, anyway. She didn't find the idea at all appealing, but then, she didn't find the idea of an entire day spent shopping appealing, either; she'd often been teased about being a disgrace to her gender.

Desperate, she tried another tack. "I'll be getting my hair done." Another ruse, she'd just gotten a trim, but worth a shot. "The smells of a salon. You'd hate it."

The grin she'd thought of before unexpectedly popped out now. "Grew up with it. My mother was a hairstylist for years."

She blinked. Distracted, she asked, "What does she do now?"

"Manage my father. Tries to manage me."

"Tries?"

The grin widened. "If I let her, she'd have nothing to complain about."

It sounded so normal, she couldn't help smiling back at him. And realized that this was Tony Alvera's real charm, not the surface teasing that made Liana call him an incurable flirt.

"I really wasn't planning on doing any of that," she confessed.

"I know."

She drew back slightly in surprise. He shrugged.

"You were just trying to scare me off."

"And with most men," she said dryly, "I would have succeeded."

"I'm not most men."

"No," she said, "you're not." And then, as the reality of their connection flooded back, she added, "You're a man on a mission."

"That, too," he said easily.

He'd meant it when he'd said he'd be glued to her for the weekend. He'd been looking forward to it, despite—or perhaps because of—the fact that it made her nervous. He wanted to probe that reaction, wanted to poke at it until she admitted again that if not for all the things that made it impossible, she'd want him.

He was editing what she'd actually said, of course, jumping ahead a step, but he didn't care. The next step would be editing out those things that made it impossible.

Yeah, right, he told himself as he drove, like you're suddenly, magically going to fit in her world?

But here he was now, on Saturday night, headed back into those mean streets. True, they had spent the day together, but it had been impossible to needle her about anything when she was working. He had a suspicion she did that a lot on her weekends; her devotion to Redstone was as deep and genuine as his own, and for similar reasons. And her focus on her work was…well, admirable, he supposed. She'd barely seemed aware he was there after she'd gone into the den, booted up her computer and logged on to her office workstation.

"Why don't you just go in to Redstone?" he finally asked when she emerged after a couple of hours for a cup of coffee.

"Because Josh told me not to on the weekends."

"So you work here instead? Do you really think that's what he meant?"

"I'm not there, am I?"

"So you're a letter-of-the-law kind of person?"

She had looked at him over the rim of the mug she was sipping from. "I am a person who owes Josh Redstone more than I can ever repay."

As am I, he'd thought.

"I thought you'd understand that," she'd said, and moments later returned to her den and her work, leaving him to spend an afternoon doing what little work he could from his cell phone, including arranging to have her car towed and repaired, and then trying again to read while the woman who seemed able to distract him from anything was in the next room.

They'd ordered in—she loved pizza, another surprise from the elegant Ms. Mercer—for dinner, and he'd met the delivery car down in the parking lot, after having given them a bogus address that was close, and his own cell number. They'd barely talked as they ate, and after they'd cleaned up—why was he working so hard to show he was domesticated?—she'd finally left her home office long enough to settle in and look at a magazine that had been in the mail he'd picked up late this morning.

A gardening magazine, he'd noted, and wondered why a woman who lived in a condo without a square foot of dirt would subscribe to such a thing.

She hasn't always lived here, he reminded himself. She'd probably lived in some huge, fashionable house with carefully landscaped grounds. He could just picture her with one of those straw garden hats he'd seen in photographs of women showing off their prized…gardenias, he finished on a sour note.

He'd been left to do nothing but try not to stare at her; she seemed determined to pretend he wasn't there.

Or rather, to treat him like what he was, her bodyguard, worthy of politeness, but nothing more.

And then just after dark Rico had called, saying he'd come up with something else. Something worth another face-to-face, and maybe, Rico had suggested, even more money than before.

He'd called in to Draven, who had sent Hill out to stay with Lilith. Tony had waited for her, and while not chewing her out as he once might have, had pointed out what she'd missed with the brake fluid. The young woman was properly chagrined, and Tony knew she'd be hypervigilant now to make up for it. Which had been his point.

She'd also handed him an envelope from Draven; paying for information was getting expensive, and he'd already given Rico most of his cash kept back for just that purpose.

"I'll be back, and then you can go home," he'd told her.

"I can stay tonight, if you want a break."

He'd nearly snapped at her then, but stopped himself, wondering what had made her say it. Her expression was utterly guileless—too guileless, he wondered?—and he finally gave it up. He was walking too close to the edge when such a simple thing could set him off, he thought.

"I'll be back," he repeated, and left.

So here he was, at nearly midnight, with a pocketful of hundreds that any number of guys likely within ten yards of him at this moment would slit his throat for without a second thought, working his way through foreign turf to what had once been his own. He'd been an ES 13 once, and that alone would have gotten him killed on Cholo turf even then; now that he was long out of the life, he had no armor at all except his own skill and training, and the instincts that were on high alert at the moment.

And the Glock 21 he'd pulled out of the hidden compartment in the panel of the driver's door of his car. It was nestled at the small of his back, a comforting presence.

He pondered, not for the first time, if this was a trap. Rico had no real loyalty to him, not since he'd left the gang, and only respect for his former membership had kept him alive before. But right now he was a cash cow for Rico, and that wasn't something the man would give up on easily.

Then again, the wad in his pocket might be thought of as a last bit of milk from that cow, after which you might as well slaughter it for the meat.

Rico had suggested an out-of-the-way building for the meet. Tony had insisted on a more public place, but still on ES 13 turf.

"You don't trust me, *vato?*" Rico had asked in indignant tones.

"As much as you trust me, *vato,*" he'd replied, earning a laugh.

He made the turn and spotted Rico, pacing rather nervously just out of the halo of light from the one unbroken streetlamp on the block.

Otherwise the street seemed deserted, but he knew better than to assume. He drove slowly but saw nothing. Rico spotted him, gestured sharply, as if urging him to hurry.

He pulled over, checked the Glock, settled it again and got out of the car, every sense tuned to his surroundings.

"Hurry up, man!"

Rico was very nervous, and the possibility of a setup went through Tony's mind again.

"You do something stupid, Rico?" he asked softly as he neared the man.

"Christ, man," Rico retorted. "You want what I got or not?"

"Talk to me."

"That friend of mine. He says that Chilton dude, he buddied up in the city jail before he got transferred to that country club place. Gave me the other guy's name. I checked him out on Google."

Tony blinked.

"What?" Rico sneered, "you think we don't got our own kind of network? Think we're stuck in the old days? You been gone too long, *pendejo*."

Tony ignored the slur on his ancestry. He had been gone a long time, but it would never be long enough, not in his mind. "And?" he prompted.

"A guy Chilton was buddied up with was the same guy they sent up for buying what Chilton was selling."

"Santerelli?"

"That's what—"

The scream of car tires on asphalt split the night. That meant only one thing in this neighborhood, and no matter how long he was away, Tony knew he'd never forget that.

Yanking out the Glock, he dove for the cover of his parked car, while Rico took off running back into the darkness. He heard the yelling from the racing car.

When the shots came, as he'd known they would, it was as if he'd never left.

Chapter 21

Lilith found herself holding her breath as Taylor closed her cell phone, breaking the connection. She made herself take in air. She already knew it had been Tony, from the side of the conversation she'd heard, but Taylor confirmed it with her first words.

"He's on his way back."

Lilith nodded, but something about the way Taylor wasn't meeting her eyes set off an alarm in her mind. That and the fact that he'd left hours ago, and that now it was nearly two in the morning. Taylor had told her to go to bed, but she hadn't even tried, knowing she wouldn't sleep.

And what that said about the state of her feelings for this man was something she wasn't sure she wanted to face.

"What is it, Taylor?"

"Nothing."

"He's a better liar than you are, and I still know," she said.

Taylor sighed. "There was…an incident."

"An 'incident'?" When Taylor didn't respond, Lilith asked, "Did he tell you not to tell me?"

"No."

"Then tell me."

Another sigh. "It was a drive-by shooting."

Again Lilith forgot to breathe. And she realized in that instant, the instant before she asked the question that could change everything, that she was face-to-face with those feelings whether she was ready or not. "Is he all right?"

Taylor blinked, as if the very idea that Tony Alvera could be hurt had never occurred to her. Was the woman naive, or did she just see him as invincible? Many thought of Redstone Security that way, she knew, and she supposed to some extent they had to think of themselves that way, to do the jobs they did.

"I...assume so," Taylor finally said. "He didn't say otherwise."

As if he would, Lilith thought. And then, belatedly, it occurred to her to ask, "Was someone else hurt?"

"Yes," Taylor said, reluctantly.

...they killed my little sister in a drive-by.

Tony's words rang in her head, and her throat tightened as she imagined how he must be feeling, no matter who it was who'd been hurt tonight.

Taylor got up off the couch where they'd been sitting, trying to watch a movie that had captured neither of them. She gathered cups and dishes—Lilith had discovered to her chagrin that Taylor shared her weakness for all things butterscotch—and carried them back to the kitchen.

Taylor would leave when Tony arrived, Lilith supposed. And then she would be facing another night with the man who so unsettled her, she didn't know whether to wish the guest bedroom had a lock on the door or be thankful it didn't.

Now she knew.

The very realization that something could have happened to him, that he could have been hurt, or worse, had brought slamming home into her mind the simple fact that she would be devastated. And no amount of telling herself she was a silly female falling for the big, strong man protecting her could change that.

Besides, she knew perfectly well that it wasn't that. She wasn't afraid, she'd never been afraid during this time, only angry. The only person who had ever been a threat to her was in prison, and she refused to live her life in fear. Doing that would mean Daniel had won, and she absolutely would not give him that satisfaction.

So where did that leave her? Besides lusting after—she couldn't kid herself about that any longer—a man twelve years her junior?

...you don't have to tell me you're out of my league, I know that.

His words came back to her, along with her sense of the absurdity of it. Her "league," as he called it, consisted of a man who hid behind the facade of refinement and upper-crust gentility, denying he would ever hurt so much as a flea, while his wife lay in the hospital bed he'd put her in. Tony Alvera had more honesty and honor in his little finger than Daniel could muster in a lifetime.

"He's pretty...intense."

Lilith snapped out of her reverie to find Taylor standing a few feet away, watching her, assessing.

"Yes," she agreed; there didn't seem any point in denying it.

Taylor seemed to hesitate, then shrugged. "You do know this was never just a job for him, right?"

Lilith frowned. "What do you mean?"

"I was in Mr. Draven's office when he burst in, demanding this assignment."

"He...what?"

"I think the boss was about to assign me, thinking you'd be more comfortable with a woman. Then Tony arrived, saying the job was his." Taylor gave her a faint smile. "I never would have thought anyone would have the nerve to talk to Mr. Draven like that."

"He's mellowed a bit," Lilith said, barely aware of her own response. The vision of Tony charging into Draven's office demanding to be the one to protect her broke down the last bit of that crumbling wall she'd tried to keep around her response to his overpowering, larger-than-life presence.

She made herself focus on the woman watching her. "Why did you tell me that?"

The shrug again. "Seems to me you're a little...conflicted about him. I thought it might help."

Lilith laughed despite herself. "Conflicted. Yes, that's a good word for it."

Or it had been, she thought. Because she wasn't sure she was in the least conflicted anymore.

When a few minutes later she heard strong, quick steps on her stairway, she let out a compressed breath. Whether it was an ebbing of worry—he was obviously well enough to move in his normal manner—or an increase in anxiety at his return, she wasn't sure.

She seemed unable to move and just stood there as Taylor and Tony held a quiet exchange in the doorway. Then the woman left, with a backward glance at her and a smile that Lilith would have sworn said "Good luck."

Lord, was it that obvious?

When Tony turned to face her, her breath shot out of her yet again; he was spattered with blood. His hands looked as if he'd been swimming in it. Instinctively she reached out to touch him.

"Are you hurt?" she asked urgently, suddenly disbelieving Taylor's earlier assurance.

He gave her an oddly assessing look before he said quietly, "It's not mine."

She stared up at him. "The man you went to see?"

He nodded.

"Is he…?"

"Dead. Yes. There was nothing I could do for him."

And he would have tried. Lilith knew that as surely as she knew he was standing here. No matter what manner of man it had been, even had he been the worst that ran those streets, Tony would have tried.

"I'm sorry. Was he…a friend?"

Tony's mouth twisted. "Once, he would have been a brother to me, simply because we both belonged to the same gang. But no, he wasn't really a friend. Didn't make it much easier to watch him die."

Lilith shook her head, slowly. "I can't imagine. It must have made you think of—"

"Yes. It did."

The edge that had come into his voice warned her to veer away from that subject. She stared at him, still unable to look away from the stains on his shirt, his hands. Finally she lifted her gaze to his face. "You're really all right?"

She didn't know what had changed in her voice to make his expression shift. But it did, and he looked down at her with a sudden ferocity that left her no doubt what he was referring to when he bit out, "No."

He reached for her, then stopped abruptly, and she saw his gaze flick from her to his bloodied hands, then back. And slowly he lowered them, but his eyes, those dark, hot eyes, told her this was only a temporary respite.

A sudden panic filled her, and she wanted nothing more than to retreat. "I'll…get you some towels, a washcloth, so you can…wash that off."

It was inane, it was so far from what she was feeling she almost laughed at herself. And half expected him to laugh out loud at her. But he let her retreat, although she again had the feeling she was only buying herself a few minutes. Something had changed about him tonight, something was there that hadn't been before, something that warned her the wolf was about to slip the leash.

She heard him in the guest bathroom, wondered what it must feel like to have to clean another human being's blood off your skin. What it must have felt like to be back on those streets where he'd grown up, once more hearing shots fired like the one that had killed his little sister.

"There's something I need to tell you."

She gave a little start; she hadn't heard him come out of the bathroom. For a big man, he moved like a cat. When she looked at his face, it was set in such grim lines her stomach knotted. He'd seen so much, done so much, she didn't want to think about what could make him look like that.

"What?" she asked, even though she was positive she didn't want to hear whatever it was.

"There was...someone, once. Nine years ago. Lisa Marquette. She was someone I'd met in college, but we ran into each other again and...hit it off."

Lilith found herself holding her breath, and had the inane thought that no one had ever interfered with her normal breathing the way this man had.

"I was working a case then. One of my first, and a nasty one. One of Redstone's marketing guys was being extorted with threats to his little boy. I knew him, he was my old boss in fact, so I was...seriously invested."

"Of course," she said when he paused.

He was silent so long she wondered if he was going to stop altogether. Wondered why he was telling her in the first place, it was so obviously painful for him. He couldn't even look at her anymore; he was staring down at the floor as if the diagonal pattern of the slate tiles was the most fascinating thing in the world.

"It got ugly," he said at last. "Very. And I couldn't seem to get a handle on it, couldn't track the suspects even though I had a decent idea who they were. Then just before it all came to a head, it became clear *they* knew who *I* was. Things got dicey, and I got…pretty wound up."

Lilith listened silently now, but with a growing curiosity as to what the two seemingly divergent stories had to do with each other.

And then he told her.

"I got wound so tight I blew up at Lisa. I couldn't talk about the case with her, but I was worried she might be in danger if they knew enough about me to follow me. So I ordered her to stay locked inside. Because I couldn't explain, she got angry in turn."

Lilith took in a shallow breath. She couldn't help thinking of her own reaction to his imperious orders. Was that what this was about, was this some convoluted apology for how he'd acted, for his high-handed manner and arrogant insistence?

"It…escalated."

His voice had dropped. Odd, she thought, that he had started this here, standing in her hallway. Odder still that he was now leaning against the wall where they stood, as if he needed the prop.

"And I didn't have time to fix it, not then. I thought I would later. I had to go out because there had been another extortion call. The call was a setup. To lure me out. She was angry enough that when I left…so did she."

He fell silent again for a long moment. His expression didn't change, nor did his own breathing, but she knew the punch line was coming.

And that it was going to be ugly.

"I don't think they meant for her to die. They just wanted to scare me off. They kidnapped her, restrained her and covered her mouth with duct tape, tossed her in the trunk of a car. The medical examiner said she…suffocated. She had gotten so scared she vomited."

Lilith shuddered, understanding what he wasn't saying. And he still wasn't looking at her. She was grateful for that, at least for a moment. She was trying to wrap her mind around the scope of the tragedy this one man had had in his life. As if living the way he'd had to as a child hadn't been enough, then the senseless death of his sister, and then...this? She couldn't imagine what it must be like to live with such memories. In her mind, they made her own painful ones seem almost clean.

Finally, slowly, he lifted his gaze to her face. "She died, horribly, because of me. Because I slipped back into the old days, the old ways, the old machismo my father lives by."

A protest rose to her lips, but she stopped it, making herself wait until she could speak calmly, gently. "It wasn't your fault, Tony."

"So they say."

"She made the decision."

"But I pushed her to it." He eyed her steadily. "Would you have stayed, if it had been your ex ordering you around?"

"No," she admitted. "But there's a big difference. Daniel would have imposed his orders with brute force. You would never do that. You would never...hurt me."

"You were angry enough, last night, to walk out. If this hadn't been your home, you might have."

She couldn't deny that, either. Didn't want to deny it. Somehow she knew honesty was imperative now; this man wouldn't want or accept any banal, insincere platitudes. This was Tony Alvera stripped down to the bone, and she didn't dare trifle with that.

"I might have. More likely I would have just thrown your sorry...backside out."

He looked startled, but the tiny beginnings of a grin tugged at the corners of his mouth.

"So next time," she said, "just ask. Don't try to bully me."

His expression shifted again, turned slightly sardonic. "Just ask?"

"If you'd just said 'Lilith, I need you to do this,' I wouldn't have fought you. And one little 'please' goes a very long way."

She studied him for a long moment before asking what she'd

wanted to know since he'd first started his grim story. "Why did you tell me this? About Lisa? Was it to explain why you acted like that the other night?"

"Partly."

"And the other part?"

"Because you should know the worst thing about me."

Her throat tightened almost unbearably. "Why?"

"Because I'm going to ask you again."

She stared up at him, knowing what he meant, knowing this was the moment she'd known was coming, the moment some part of her had been thinking about even as she tried to force it out of her conscious mind.

"Only this time," he said, with a quiet acknowledgment and admission that was as much apology as anything else, "it has nothing to do with my job."

"I...see."

"I hope so. So once more...your bed, or that silly bunk bed?"

She'd wondered how it would feel, to make this decision. Now she knew she wouldn't find out, because on some level, some part of her mind, the decision had already been made.

"You can say it better than that, Mr. Alvera."

She thought she heard him suck in a breath. And then a slow grin curved his mouth, making that unexpected dimple flash. There was nothing of the practiced charm in this, only the genuine, unexpected sweetness she'd seen sparks of before. And when he spoke, it was with a voice so full of gentle teasing and boyish dutifulness that she nearly grinned back at him.

"Lilith, I need you to do this. Please."

"All right, then," she said.

And the moment she spoke the words, the instant she saw the heat flare in his eyes, she knew she'd taken an irrevocable step. She might someday regret it, the impossibilities were all still there, but right now, as he pulled her into his arms and lowered his mouth to hers, she truly didn't care.

Chapter 22

He'd known it would be sweet. He'd known it would be hot. He'd even known, on some level, that it would be unlike anything he'd ever experienced.

But he hadn't known it would be like this. Because he hadn't known *anything* could be like this.

The moment he realized she was trembling, he reined himself in with one of the fiercest efforts of his life. He undressed her gently, letting out the tender side of what he was feeling, the emotions that he had no words for. He wanted her now, right now, but he also wanted her for the rest of his life, and he wasn't going to get that if he scared her, rushed her now. Even with her bed right here, a step away, he had to go slow.

When she tentatively reached for him, helped him tug off his shirt, his belly tightened fiercely, knotting with a heat and tension he'd never felt before. He treasured every move she made, every quickened breath she took, every tiny sign that she wanted him, too. He had to fight down the urge to take her now, hard and fast, before she could change her mind.

He'd wondered if her concern about the difference in their ages was based on something more than the calendar, if it stemmed from what she saw in the mirror every day. He'd known he wouldn't care—the thought of looking, of having the right to look, at her naked body, in a mirror or otherwise, told him that—but he'd made up his mind she wouldn't care, either. As it turned out, he didn't have to work very hard at it.

She was beautiful. As beautiful as he'd imagined. More. In a womanly way, with luscious, taut curves that made his fingers curl with the urge to trace every one. He'd meant to tell her he thought she was just that. Now that it was here, now that she stood before him, he couldn't say a word.

But when he lifted a hand to touch her, he saw he was trembling himself, and had to hope that that would tell her what he couldn't find the words to say.

He stopped, unable to move his hand that last, critical inch. In this final moment, when what he'd ached for for so long was within reach, all he could see were those faintly lighter patches across his knuckles.

I shouldn't even touch you, he thought, frozen, staring at his own past as if it were alive and here.

He didn't realize he'd spoken the words, whispered them aloud, until she followed the line of his gaze, then looked back at his face.

"I had them removed," he said, "but that doesn't change—"

He sucked in a breath as she touched him, traced those reminders on his skin with gentle fingers.

"Badges of honor," she said softly. "A permanent reminder of the courage and determination it took to get out. You should be proud."

He swallowed tightly. And he of the quick repartee, the easy flirtation, still couldn't think of a thing to say to her that didn't sound hollow and false to his ears.

Finally, he went with a gut-level truth that left him feeling as if he'd bared his throat to a blade.

"The only thing I want more than you right now, is for you to be sure."

"I'm sure," she whispered. "I've been sure since that endless second before I knew you were all right."

He wasn't sure exactly what she meant, but was positive he didn't care. He leaned forward and kissed the top of her shoulder, the spot he'd seen her rubbing on occasion, where it was no doubt sore from her near fall on the stairs.

He'd get to the other sore spot, that beautiful, lusciously curved backside, later.

He touched her then, cupped and lifted her breasts just as he'd imagined so many times. But the reality far surpassed the fantasy; the feel of that soft fullness rounding into his hands sent a jolt of fire through him that left him reeling, and wondering if there would be anything left of him but ash when this was over.

He rubbed his thumbs over her nipples. They hardened and she let out a gasping moan. The sound and feel answered his own question; there would be nothing left and he didn't care. He couldn't think of any way he'd rather go out than with this woman in his arms.

She reached for him then, urging him to shed the rest of his clothes.

"You do it," he said harshly. "I don't want to let go."

He caressed her again, savoring the way she moved at his touch, arching, shifting restlessly. When he felt her hands slide across his belly, fingers reaching for the buttons of his jeans, he sucked in a breath so quickly it was audible.

She stopped.

He was so achingly hard he thought he would die right here and now if he didn't have her hands on him soon.

"Lilith," he whispered, the first time he'd spoken her name since they'd come into her bedroom.

"I…it's been a long time."

"I know. Just don't stop."

Freed of his clothes at last, he had a moment to be aware of the contrast between them, her creamy skin and his own darker bronze. He saw her look at his hand on her, wondered if she was thinking the same thing. But then she smiled, a soft, wondering smile, and slid her own hands down to his hips, pulling him toward her. Rigid flesh met soft curve, and his usually agile brain went into free fall.

And suddenly nothing was as he'd expected, or thought it would be. Elegant, poised, collected Lilith Mercer responded fiercely, arching to him, her muscles fairly rippling beneath his touch. And she touched in turn, exploring until he was gritting his teeth with the effort to hold back. But she stroked, caressed, with just a hint of tentativeness that reminded him it had been a very long time for her.

It was a reminder he needed, to keep himself slowed down. And he wanted to go slow, wanted to trace every single, glorious inch of her. He wanted her with him every step of the way, wanted her to want it as ragingly as he did, and set about making sure that happened. He set his jaw against the urgent demand of a body so hard he thought he might die from it, and coaxed her to the edge again and again, until he was certain.

And then she was urging him on. He slipped a testing finger between her legs and found her hot and slick and ready, and the anticipation of easing this damned ache in her sweet heat was more than he could resist.

When he began to inch into her he thought she cried out; he couldn't be sure because her name ripped from somewhere low and deep in his chest. It was a long, nerve-wrenching slide as her unaccustomed body adjusted to take him, but once he was in her to the hilt, only one word echoed in his pleasure-drugged mind.

Home.

He knew in that instant he wasn't going to be able to go slow. He of the infinite control and careful uninvolvement was lost.

"I can't," he whispered to her. "Sorry, I can't go slow."

"Don't. Oh, please, don't," she said, breathlessly, stunning him more than a little.

He began to move, savoring every tiny sound she made, every lifting movement that drove him deeper. And just when he knew he couldn't hold out another instant, he heard her cry out, and felt the first clenching squeeze of her muscles around him. He let go then, slamming into her twice more, and then a shout of gasping triumph broke from him as his body erupted in an explosion of pure, sweet pleasure.

And when she held on to him, even when he would have moved to relieve her of his weight, he thought again of that single word.

Home.

When she awoke, he was gone.

She supposed she should have seen the inevitability of that. What had happened between them last night had probably been ordinary to him. Not that she doubted he'd truly wanted her. There was no way she could question that, not after the way he'd held her, touched her, and taken so long to caress her she'd almost screamed at him to finish it.

She'd expected something hot and fast. She'd gotten instead a tenderness and gentle insistence that had steadily pushed her higher than she'd ever gone in her life.

She'd expected demands and fierceness. She'd gotten soft, sweet persuasion and looks of such wonder she almost forgot all about the fact that her body was twelve years older than his, with all the extra wear and tear that entailed.

She'd also expected a casual aftermath, from a man much more experienced in this sort of thing than she was. That, she had apparently gotten.

She resisted—barely—the urge to curl her satiated body up in the fetal position to ponder what she'd done, to open the door to the morning-after regrets she sensed were hovering just on the edge of her consciousness.

But how could she regret something that had been so overpoweringly glorious? How could she regret waking up feeling like a woman who had been loved to within an inch of her life?

How could she regret the simple fact that never again would she think of Daniel first when she thought of the few men she'd shared a bed with?

Then something else that had been hovering finally penetrated the fog: coffee. She was smelling coffee.

On the thought she heard footsteps. And then he was there, in the doorway, painted dark and golden by the morning light. Beautiful, tall, strong and unabashedly naked. She watched him walk toward her, two mugs of steaming coffee in his hands. It gave her the chance to really look at him, in a way she hadn't been able to in the dark of the night.

He moved, she thought, like that big cat he'd put her in mind of last night. She supposed that was because he was so perfectly put together. Her cheeks heated as she noted the dusting of hair on his chest, remembering the rough caress of it against her nipples, and the way it had made her arch her back, wanting more. And the small patch of beard beneath the center of his lower lip made her smile; she'd never even kissed a man with so much as a mustache before.

He reached the bed too soon; she'd wanted to keep looking, to work up the nerve to give that part of him that had driven her to madness last night more than a quick glance. Not that she needed to; she knew all she needed to know—he fit her perfectly.

He sat on the edge of the bed and held out one of the mugs to her. It was, she noticed as she took it, exactly as she liked it, just enough milk to take it from near black to creamy brown.

She was grateful for the distraction, since she had absolutely no idea what to say to him. *Thanks for the most amazing night of my life* seemed a bit cliché.

And all the thoughts that she supposed inevitably followed a night like last night were now tumbling around in her head, the most prominent being *Where do we go from here?*

Assuming, of course, they went anywhere except straight back to business.

Even as she thought it, he did just that.

"I'm going to go see Joe Santerelli."

She blinked. "Now?"

He nodded. "It's Sunday. He'll be…relaxed."

"Unsuspecting, you mean," she said, thinking she was oddly thankful he'd not started by talking about last night. Realizing he'd probably done it on purpose, sensing her unease.

"If you like," he agreed easily. Then, with a touch of wariness, he added, "You're not going."

"I wasn't planning to. I never met the man. I wouldn't be of any use."

He looked relieved. "You were, with your ex," he admitted. "It was me who blew that."

"I…appreciated the way you treated him. He deserved it. It did me good to see it."

He smiled. "In that case, I forgive myself."

She hesitated, then asked what had been bothering her all night. "Last night—" he tensed, and she realized he thought she was going to bring up what had happened between them, in this bed, and quickly went on "—are you sure the man who died was really the target?"

He relaxed, and she realized how out of whack things were when talking of a drive-by shooting where someone had died was easier than talking of a night of passion. Out-of-control passion, yes, but still…

"Yeah. They were Cholos, a rival gang, and they yelled his

name. They were after him. He knew it—he'd been acting twitchy."

"Oh." It seemed wrong, to be relieved, but she was.

He took a sip of coffee, then said briskly, "Hill is on her way over."

Uh-oh, Lilith thought. Here we go. But she tried to keep her response calm, reasoned. "I'm just going to stay here this morning, do some work."

"Fine."

"I'm sure Taylor will be glad to get her Sunday morning back."

He frowned. "She's still coming."

"I don't need a babysitter."

"You're getting one."

She tried to ignore the high-handedness. "In fact, Taylor would be a distraction, since I do need to work."

"I'll tell her to leave you alone."

"That would be rude."

"Rude," he snapped, "is a word that only works in your world. And you're not in your world at the moment, you're in mine."

Just like that it was between them again, that barrier between worlds he couldn't seem to get past. And now, looking at him, at that lovely expanse of golden skin over taut muscle, she wondered if she truly had lost her mind. Because the morning light only brought home the reality that she'd dodged last night.

And she guessed the morning light was bringing home the reality to him as well, showing the faint lines around her eyes and mouth that advertised the difference in their ages.

"Did you think," she asked, her voice tight, "that because we slept together, you now own me?"

"I thought," he said, his jaw set, "that you would agree to letting me keep you safe. But your agreement isn't required."

"Back to ordering instead of asking, are we?" she snapped.

Of course, he'd gotten her into bed, so now maybe he thought it wasn't necessary anymore. But the fact that he had reverted to the very behavior he'd confessed he felt had gotten Lisa killed bothered her more than she cared to admit. Because it told her she was in this much deeper than she'd allowed herself to acknowledge.

And there's no one to blame but yourself.

The problem wasn't just the difference in their ages, although she felt that more than ever this morning. She drew herself up, refusing to clutch at the bedcovers to hide behind; it seemed ridiculously pointless after the night they'd spent.

"I can tolerate a great deal," she said quietly. "I can even tolerate overprotectiveness. What I can't tolerate is someone making the same mistake over and over again."

She got up then and escaped to the bathroom, where she tried valiantly not to weep and succeeded, for the most part.

When she finally emerged, Taylor was sitting at her kitchen bar and Tony was gone. Lilith put on a smile with that practiced ease her world—and her life with Daniel—had taught her.

Maybe Tony was right. She belonged there, in that world.

Because she certainly wasn't doing very well venturing into his.

For at least the fifth time since he'd left the condo, Tony had to force himself to focus on what he was going to say to the disgraced, imprisoned CEO of JetCal. His mind kept wanting to go backward, and no amount of telling himself Lilith was just being stubborn could erase the sting of her last words.

What I can't tolerate is someone making the same mistake over and over again.

The words stung because there was no denying the truth of them. He had done exactly what had set her off before. If it were only that, it would be bad enough. But it wasn't.

Because he'd done exactly what had sent Lisa out of their apartment to be kidnapped and die.

Again.

He tried to tell himself it was because he was worried, and that made him edgy. That much was true. He even admitted he'd reacted that way for the same reasons, that desperate need to keep the woman he loved safe.

The woman he loved...

It didn't even hit him with a jolt. He'd gone into this knowing he was halfway there already, but he'd counted on the impossibility of it, the hopelessness of trying to blend her world and his, to keep the feelings at bay, to keep him at that harmless halfway point.

It hadn't worked. And he knew that he'd been beyond that point even before last night; that incredible, powerful, life-changing night that he suspected had been as intense as it had been because he was in love with her.

And maybe that was why he was taking so long to learn, to stop himself from reacting from the gut, making the same mistake with her he'd made with Lisa. He'd never loved anybody like this before and it was distracting him.

None of which changes a damned thing, he told himself.

The minimum-security facility where Joe Santerelli was being held was much different from Chino, where Daniel Huntington was. And Santerelli was going to get out a lot sooner. Sooner than Stan Chilton as well, since Chilton had threatened lives and Santerelli had only been convicted of cooking his own books; buying industrial secrets, suborning corporate espionage was a nebulous area to convict anyone on. But Redstone influence was huge and Josh had a lot of friends, and the investigation into other areas of JetCal had netted its CEO a home away from home for quite some time.

It was also why Tony thought approaching Santerelli was the way to go; the man had a lot more to lose and therefore could be pressured. He'd already run afoul of Redstone when he'd thought he'd get away with something he told himself every businessman did, and Tony hoped he'd want to avoid that mistake again.

Of course, if he was behind the plot against Lilith, Josh would want to crush him.

You're going to have to get in line behind me, boss, he thought.

Tony watched carefully as Santerelli walked toward him. He was short and a bit rotund, although Tony guessed he'd lost a bit of weight since he'd been inside, given the way his clothes hung on him. He also walked with a hint of a strut; it had likely been a swagger when he'd started, but prison life—even at what were laughingly called country-club prisons—would take some of that out of just about anyone. Especially someone used to living large, as Santerelli had been.

Tony had asked them not to tell the man who he was, just a visitor. He didn't have many, they said, family and his attorney mostly. And as usual, the Redstone name got him what he wanted.

Tony saw the man's forehead crease when he saw him. Trying to figure out who he was, Tony guessed. Saw the puzzlement change to a frown, and guessed the man's thought process had gone from wondering who this was to realizing what he looked like. He'd chosen his clothes carefully for this visit, forgoing his usual for the kind of street attire Rico had died in last night. And he saw Santerelli realize it, saw the sudden wariness in his demeanor as he sat across the outdoor picnic table from him.

"Do I know you?"

The attitude fit, too. Imperious, superior, just like the head of some medium-wanting-to-be-big company speaking to someone he didn't think could be any help to him. Tony couldn't help but contrast this man with Josh, who treated everyone with the same respect he demanded. The respect that kept Redstone at the top of any list of best places to work, the respect that meant Josh had never had to face a group of disgruntled employees.

"You don't," Tony finally answered when Santerelli began to look uncomfortable. "But I know you. My brothers on the street, they know you."

He wasn't sure Santerelli was smart enough to pick up the hint, but the way he pulled back slightly told Tony he must have. But he pretended ignorance anyway.

"I don't know what you're talking about."

"I think you do."

"I have no idea. What is it you want?"

The still imperious tone told Tony he wasn't scared. Yet.

"The job got trickier. You're not paying enough."

Santerelli's frown deepened. "Trickier?"

And there it was, Tony thought. Of all the things Santerelli could have said, that was the one that convinced Tony he was on the right track. Not "What job?" or "Paying?" as anyone truly ignorant would have said.

"It's going to cost your little cabal more."

"We already—" He stopped, as if realizing what he was about to admit.

"Paid? Yes. But not enough."

"I don't know what you're talking about," he said again.

Tony had had enough of the silly game. "It might be wiser if you did."

The frown again. "Wiser?"

Tony stood up. Heightwise he towered over the shorter man, and the contrast was even greater with Santerelli seated. He put his palms flat on the table and leaned in, letting every bit of the menace he was feeling toward this man show in his body language, his face, and his voice. The man reacted before he even spoke, quailing slightly, pulling back.

"Stealing from Redstone was one thing," Tony said icily. "Trying to hurt one of the family, and a close personal friend of Josh Redstone himself, that's something else."

"Redstone?"

The gulped exclamation said it all, and Tony finally saw what he'd wanted to see—fear.

"What do you have to do with Redstone?"

"I," Tony said, leaning in, "am the man who will decide if you simply continue to serve your time here in relative peace, forgotten as you deserve, or if the entire force of Redstone comes down on you."

Santerelli squirmed on the seat. Tony knew in that instant the man would break.

"If you think he can't make your life a living hell even in here, you're wrong."

He paused, then leaned in even farther, until he was barely inches from Santerelli's face, sensing the man was on the edge. He had no qualms about what he was going to say next, not after this man had conspired to hurt or kill a woman he didn't even know.

His woman.

Lilith.

Because she was his woman, even if he would never in his life have any more than he'd had last night.

"You have a wife, Santerelli. A son."

The man paled. He squeaked. He literally squeaked, before managing to get any words out. "You…wouldn't."

"Josh would never countenance hurting them. It's not his way. And it would put him on your level, hurting an innocent to get to someone else."

Santerelli took a breath, clearly relieved. The man wasn't just a coward, Tony thought, he was a fool. But it was the cowardice that was going to get him what he wanted right now.

"*Josh* wouldn't," he said ominously. "But I run on different rules."

Panic slammed into the man, visibly. Santerelli looked around wildly, as if for help.

"No help here. If you want to wake up from this nightmare, there's only one way to do it. Tell me everything."

Santerelli broke.

Chapter 23

Lilith looked at her reflection in the mirror. Again. She wasn't one for overindulgence in checking her own appearance, but this morning she seemed driven to it. As if what she'd done must have forever imprinted itself on her face.

But there was no sign, except for a new weariness in her eyes, that she was forever changed. The reflection that looked back at her was the same; younger than she was on the calendar, and much younger than she felt just now. She had always been passingly grateful that she didn't look her age; now she wasn't sure it was a blessing. If she did, she might not be in this painful place now.

"You knew," she whispered to herself. "You knew you shouldn't, and you did it anyway."

She made herself turn away and start to dress. She'd already spent enough time hiding in her bathroom, and too much just standing there doing nothing. Even the simple decision to take a shower had seemed too difficult; did she want to wash away any trace of Tony Alvera, or savor the scent of him on her skin because that was all she had left?

She wondered what had happened to her usual calm, decisive self, wondered if she had been burned away last night, replaced by that eager, hungry woman she didn't even recognize.

Hungry for a man who, in his way, was as high-handed as Daniel had been?

She'd assumed the biggest barrier between them was her age, or his own hangup about the differences between their worlds. She'd never thought it would be this. Although she knew perfectly well that Tony's actions stemmed from genuine concern, and not Daniel's bone-deep need for total control, she wasn't sure how much it mattered if the end result was the same.

"Ms. Mercer? Are you all right?"

Taylor's voice came through the closed door. She supposed the young woman thought she'd slipped and fallen in the shower, she'd been in here so long.

"I'm fine, Taylor. I'll be out in a few minutes."

She moved hurriedly then, dressing in faded, comfortably soft jeans and a Redstone shirt that made her feel somehow stronger.

"There's a cinnamon bagel left," Taylor said as she came into the kitchen for the second time; the first time she'd lasted only long enough to determine Tony was really gone before retreating to the bathroom, mumbling about taking a shower.

"Thank you," Lilith said. It sounded as perfunctory as it was, and she added with more life, "I like cinnamon bagels."

"I remembered," Taylor said, and Lilith recalled then that she had mentioned it when they discovered their mutual butterscotch addiction.

She warmed and ate the bagel, then went into her Saturday routine, general tidying up, sorting mail that had accumulated, cleaning the kitchen. Normally she would have stripped the bed by now and tossed the sheets into the laundry, but she hadn't. Somehow making that decision was even harder than the decision to take a shower.

She nearly laughed aloud at herself, and the only thing that stopped her was the realization that explaining it to Taylor would be impossible.

"So, how long have you and Tony been together?"

Lilith whirled, nearly dropping the plate she'd been about to put into the dishwasher. Lord, did it show after all? Was it somehow obvious that she'd spent the night having passionate, wild sex with a passionate, wild man she had no business being with?

"I beg your pardon?" she asked when she could speak.

Taylor blushed. "I'm sorry, I don't mean to pry. It's none of my business."

Lilith steadied herself. She didn't want to ask, had to ask. "What makes you think we're 'together' at all?"

The younger woman blinked. "Uh...superhot chemistry?" It was Lilith's turn to blink. Taylor shrugged then, before adding, "I mean, seriously, you two, like...sizzle. So I assumed..."

Seized by an urge she tried and failed to combat, Lilith took advantage of likely the most unbiased opinion she could get on the matter. "Don't you think we'd be a bit of an...odd couple?"

Taylor gave her a sideways look. "I don't know either of you that well."

"I meant...appearancewise." At Taylor's wary look, she added, "It's all right. I really want to know."

"Odd?" Taylor repeated, as if considering the word. "No. Dramatic, yes. Head turning. Opposites attract and all, I guess. I mean, he's dark and you're so fair, he's exotic, you're classic. Both beautiful, but different." She smiled then. "I think you look amazing together."

And there you have it, Lilith thought. Not a word about what bothered either of them the most.

With the feeling there was a lesson there, Lilith turned back to her chores.

And wondered why Taylor's observations didn't make anything seem any easier.

"So Chilton and Santerelli hatched this together?"

Tony looked away from his hands, where the paler spots along the knuckles showed where he'd once worn the badge of the ES 13s. He raised his gaze to Draven, who was leaning on the edge of his desk at the airport hangar office of Redstone Security. "Yes."

"This was their idea of taking revenge on Redstone? Hurting or killing someone who had nothing to do with their downfall?"

"Apparently so." Tony grimaced; the knowledge that Lilith had been in genuine danger still made him queasy. Afraid of what he might betray to the too perceptive Draven, he added quickly, "But then, if they were smart, they would never have tried to spy on Redstone to begin with."

"Truer words never spoken," Draven said. "Well, at least it's over now. Our end, anyway, the officials can handle it from here. Good job, Tony. I'll let Josh know."

"Yes."

It's over. Truer words never spoken.

Funny how just a change in sentence order spoke an even more definite truth.

Because it was over. It had to be. He looked again at the discoloration on his hands, thought of the one he couldn't see, at the back of his neck.

If he'd had half the class Lilith had, he would have stopped last night. He would have stopped the moment he'd glanced down and seen these hands on her creamy, delicate skin. But he'd been wild with need, and then she'd touched him back, as if she thought his darker, scarred skin was as beautiful as her own, and he'd been lost.

Badges of honor, she'd called those marks, the faint discolorations and the actual scars. Badges of courage, and determination.

Maybe. But that didn't move him into her world. Nothing could do that. You had to be born into it.

"What's brewing?" he said suddenly. "There must be something on your plate by now."

"Where?" Draven asked, looking as startled as he was capable of looking.

"Anywhere." Draven frowned. Tony dug in. "I want to work. Send me somewhere. The farther away the better."

"You just got back from Caracas, then Beck's case and before that you spent months in the jungle in Brazil. Then you jumped right into this. Don't you want a break, or at least to stay home for a while?"

Home. Right. He'd found home last night, in Lilith's arms. Problem was, it wasn't *his* home. And if he tried to make it home, he'd just end up making her angry all over again, eventually.

What I can't tolerate is someone making the same mistake over and over again....

That, he thought bitterly, would be me. "No. There must be something, somewhere. Didn't you mention Australia a while back?"

"Yes, but that's all done except for the mop-up."

"Fine. Let me do the mop-up."

"Australia?"

"Perfect," Tony said, thinking that the entire planet between him and Lilith might just be enough.

"Why don't you just take a vacation?" Draven suggested dryly.

"I'd rather work. But either way, I want out of here."

Back in his apartment overlooking the harbor full of expensive boats—a place he'd consciously chosen so that every day he would remember how far he'd come—he began to toss things into his battered suitcase; the trip to Austria and that mess in the village near the Redstone ski resort in Innsbruck four years ago had been hard on the thing.

It had been hard on him, too; skiing and the cold had never been in his repertoire, and he'd rarely felt so out of place as he had there. His cover had been a visiting, wealthy playboy of unspecified Latin descent, and he'd played it to the hilt, the facade the only thing that let him function at an altitude intimidating in reality and in his mind.

He was, he realized, thinking about such things to avoid thinking about what was in fact taking up most of his mind. The realization that he was running came as a bit of a shock. And from a woman. He who had never run from anything or anyone in his life, and had the scars to prove it, was running like a scared kid.

But then, it was the scars, both physical and otherwise, that were the reason he was running. Because he couldn't deny any longer that Lisa's death had scarred him in ways he hadn't even understood until Lilith.

"Think about something else, damn it!"

That he'd said it out loud, to an empty room, nearly made him groan. But he tried to follow his own order anyway.

He should be feeling satisfied at the quick wrap-up to this case. Draven had been pleased, at least. The fact that he *didn't* feel satisfied was just further proof that he'd gotten in way over his head. It was over—all of it—and the best thing he could do was get himself out of Lilith's life and on with his own.

Such as it would be, now that he'd had a taste—God, such a sweet, hot, incredible taste—of her.

It's over, he repeated as he tossed a pair of socks into the bag. As soon as Draven called to say that the flight was arranged, he'd be on his way, leaving the wheels of Redstone to grind Chilton up for him.

And then there it was again, that niggling feeling that he'd missed something, that there was something that just didn't feel right about the whole thing. It wasn't that it had been too easy—cases actually were easy, sometimes—but something else, something he couldn't quite bury.

You just wanted it to be her ex-husband, he told himself sourly. Or worse, you're just looking for any excuse to see her again.

And neither would change anything. However good they'd been together—and the passion that had exploded had shocked even him—it was still impossible. She clearly knew that, it was him who was having the problem swallowing the inevitable.

But he couldn't seem to let it go.

When he caught himself standing over the open suitcase with a shirt in his hand, uncertain how long he'd been there staring into space, everything that had happened in the last week tumbling through his mind, he swore under his breath.

He tossed down the shirt and began to pace, needing the physical movement to try and get a grip. But it didn't work, and before long, even knowing he was likely being seven kinds of an idiot, he was sitting at his notebook computer, logging on to the Redstone network and pulling up the report he'd filed just hours earlier.

He read through it all again. He sat for a while, staring at a rushing, star field screen saver as if the answer was somehow there in that random pattern.

Then he made two phone calls, one to Redstone's in-house tech genius, Ryan Barton, who quickly found and e-mailed him the software program he'd written at Draven's request a few months ago; Tony had used it, but hadn't yet installed it on his home computer.

The second was to a woman he knew at the county sheriff's office. She was his most reliable unofficial source, had been since the day she had laughingly told him he'd get a lot further with her if he turned off the automatic flirting device and simply asked.

So next time, just ask. Don't try to bully me.

Lilith's words echoed in his head. He *had* tried to bully her, since he couldn't bring himself to try and charm her, not when he knew how superficial, how shallow those efforts were. Not when he knew how she despised the tactic, thanks to her ex-husband.

"Is that what you wanted?"

Tony yanked himself out of the reverie and read back the data she had given him.

"Yes," he said, "thanks."

"Just dates? That's all you need?"

"That's all," Tony said absently, hanging up without really saying goodbye, his eyes scanning the numbers he'd scrawled on the notepad.

He called up the newly installed program Ryan had sent him. He entered the dates he'd just gotten. Then he switched to his own report, took the dates and locations from there and entered those as well. There were a lot of them, so it took a while. Then he activated the program's compare function and waited.

Nothing. No match, no correlation that hadn't already come to him and been checked out.

For a moment he sat there, telling himself to give it up, that his instincts couldn't be relied on when his heart kept interfering, making him want to look for something that wasn't there. He got up and started pacing again, shaking his head at himself; he felt edgier than he could ever remember, since he'd left the streets.

Maybe he was simply losing his mind.

But then something else struck him, that he hadn't entered quite all the data he'd collected. He got up, went over to the half-packed suitcase, where he'd tossed his jacket. He dug into the pocket for the small notebook he used to scribble notes in. Primitive, yes, but for some things he still preferred media that could be literally burned afterward.

He found what he'd been looking for, entered it into the program, made one more call for one more date and entered that. Then he ran the program again.

In moments, a single line of data in common appeared in the search box. A single line consisting of a date, a time and a place.

A single line that changed everything.

Chapter 24

The anger he'd felt when confronting Joe Santerelli was nothing compared to what he was feeling now. Stan Chilton's betrayal was so much worse, because he'd been Redstone.

Tony would be willing to bet you could count on one hand the number of bad apples that had slipped through since the founding of Redstone. Josh's instincts about people were rarely wrong. It was part of what had changed him from a young man with nothing more than drive and a plan into the head of a multinational corporation that dwarfed most privately held companies in the world. He'd built Redstone into something that to those who didn't understand seemed impossible: even a total stranger was family if they were Redstone.

And Stan Chilton had turned on that family.

He was where he belonged because of it, but that wasn't good enough for Tony right now.

When he was brought out, Chilton took one look at Tony and stopped. He tried to tell the guard he didn't want this visitor, tried to turn back, but the man was already gone. The Redstone name reached even here; Josh believed fully in supporting his local police. And since Redstone was just about everywhere, that was a lot of support.

"Who are you?" Chilton asked, a quaver in his voice.

"Redstone," Tony said simply.

Chilton drew back, eyes widening as he gave Tony a fearful look up and down. Tony knew he had him then. And it was a matter of only minutes before he had the confirmation he needed.

Next stop, Chino, he thought.

When he was face-to-face with Daniel Huntington again, Tony realized that he'd long ago surpassed anger. He was enraged. He wanted the pure, physical pleasure of his hands around this man's throat. And he didn't bother to hide it as the urbane, elegant man clad in the baggy jumpsuit sat down. He had the satisfaction of seeing a touch of wariness mar Huntington's supercilious expression. And although Huntington's words belied it, Tony didn't forget it.

"Well, well. If it isn't my wife's pit bull."

Tony didn't rise to the bait this time. "I don't work for your *ex*-wife."

Huntington lifted a brow. "No? Then who? Whoever's screwing her at the moment?"

Tony grinned, knowing it would infuriate the man. "It must really humiliate you to realize you weren't man enough for her." He remembered the man's own words. "You're less than nothing to her."

Huntington swore crudely, cracking the smooth facade for a moment. And with a sudden flash of insight, Tony realized something about the first time he'd seen this man. He remembered the moment when he'd seen fear flicker in Huntington's eyes. The moment when he'd seen Lilith, in her purposefully chosen pose, seated as relaxed and casually as if she were sitting in a friend's living room. As if he didn't bother her at all.

That flash of fear hadn't been of him. It had been of Lilith. Because she hadn't been afraid of him anymore.

And Tony knew he could break him, here and now.

"Of course," he said with a laughing contempt he knew would rankle beyond anything else, "any man would be more man than you are, you twisted, useless—no, wait. I'm sure you have your uses in here."

"We're done," Huntington snapped, starting to rise.

"Like hell we are," Tony said. "Sit. Down. Like the bitch you are. And if you think I can't make sure you're used like one by half the inmates here, think again. All your money won't save your sorry ass."

Huntington was naturally pale, but Tony didn't think he was wrong in thinking the man just went a shade lighter. And he sat.

"Who are you?"

There was more than a touch of wariness in Huntington's voice now, there was fear along with the confusion. Tony could smell it. He could smell it, with instincts honed on the dangerous streets where smelling another's fear could be the one thing that kept you alive. This man was an amateur in this world, and a coward in his own.

"I'm the man who's going to haunt you until your dying day. You'll never be free of me. You'll never again take an unworried breath. Ever. Because I'll be there. Every time you turn around."

He knew he probably looked like Huntington's worst nightmare. Should have kept the tats, he thought, knowing the sight of spidery gang tattoos would have sent Huntington over the edge a lot quicker.

But then a sudden memory of Lilith last night, tracing the faintly lighter places on his skin, declaring them badges of honor, shot through his mind. The image of her, delicate, fair, beautiful, in the arms of a man wearing the declarations of the life that would have eventually killed him, was impossible, and he'd never been more glad he'd had them removed.

Huntington's fear was rapidly escalating, and Tony pressed.

"I have resources you can't even begin to imagine. Your own are nothing compared to mine. And I'll use them all against you. You can't hide. There's no place you can go that I can't find you."

"Who *are* you?" The fear was uppermost now, above even the confusion.

"I'm Redstone."

Huntington blinked. His puzzlement vanished, but the fear only increased. Good, thought Tony.

"Yes," he said. "Be afraid. Very afraid."

"I'm not—"

"Then you should be."

"Why? Is my wife sleeping with Josh Redstone now? I always suspected there was more to that—"

Again, with an effort, Tony didn't rise to the bait. "You should be afraid because being Redstone makes my life so much easier. I don't have any of those annoying rules to follow. I don't have a civilian board looking over my shoulder all the time, no one to scream about brutality, or to care if you end up in the hospital. Or worse. And I have a boss who cares about results and won't second-guess my methods. But then, you know that."

Tony was guessing that Huntington knew quite well the reputation of Redstone, and of their security team. He'd been a mover and shaker at nearly the same level; he'd know how much pressure Redstone could bring to bear.

"What you don't know is that I came from exactly where you think I came from. A place where life is cheap and payback is truly hell."

"You can't come in here—"

"Yet I have. Because the Redstone name will get me in anywhere. And once I'm there, the game is played by my rules."

"What do you want?" Fear was gaining the upper hand, Tony noted with satisfaction.

"My rules," Tony said in a near whisper, "say you get more than what you ask for. Not an eye for an eye, but an eye for an eyelash. And for attempted murder…"

He let the words trail off, saw Huntington's eyes widen, saw him suck in a gasping breath at the clear implication.

"I owe Josh Redstone my life." Tony went for that fear. He lowered his voice again. "I would *kill* for Josh Redstone."

A tiny whimper broke from Huntington, and Tony guessed what he was feeling had shown in his face. "Call for a guard, and I'll do it right here and now."

He was trusting the man was scared enough not to realize that a visitor committing murder here was insane. Or that Huntington believed Tony was just that, insane. The man was trembling now, a barely perceptible shiver beneath the urbane exterior, but it was there.

"You made four crucial mistakes, Huntington. First, you're a bigot who assumed anyone in prison, especially if they're Mexican, had the capacity to commit murder for hire. Second, you chose incompetents—but then, how would you know, when you don't even realize how incompetent you yourself are?"

Huntington's temper flared. At the accusation of incompetence, Tony noted, not of murder for hire.

"Go to hell."

"From where I sit, you're the one in hell. But where you are now is paradise compared to where you're going."

"You can't—"

"Third," Tony ticked off on his fingers. "You went after someone who matters to Josh Redstone. And he is a man who knows the meaning of friendship and loyalty. A man who wouldn't hesitate to use every bit of the worldwide power he holds to defend one of his own. He'll crush you, your reputation, and toss the debris into the sewer where it belongs."

The bluster vanished. Huntington was starting to look like the cornered rat he was. Tony got up and walked around the table. He sat down next to Huntington, who tried to scuttle away sideways on the bench. Tony clamped his fingers on the back of the man's neck, wondering if he would have the willpower not to break it.

"But your worst mistake," he whispered, so close to Huntington's ear, "was crossing me."

Huntington whimpered again, trying to pull away. Tony tightened his grip, thinking how easy it would be to snap the vertebrae beneath his fingers. But death was too clean, too easy for this man. He deserved worse.

His worst nightmares come true.

"I have brothers in this place, *pendejo*. Lots of them. And unlike the bumblers you hired, they *have* killed. They're in for life already, and they have nothing to lose."

"What do you want?" This time the question was a plea, and Tony knew Huntington was crumbling. But he didn't stop.

"You'll never know which ones they are, or when I'll tell them to strike. And they won't kill you right away. They'll just torture you. And I don't mean that pansy-ass stuff you people think of as torture. I mean the real thing."

"What do you want, damn you? A confession?"

"I'm not the police. I don't need a confession. And your partners already rolled on you. Not only did you pick incompetents to try to kill her, you chose cowards as your accomplices. Santerelli and Chilton couldn't wait to toss it all in your lap."

"Santerelli?" Huntington looked genuinely blank, but Tony had expected that.

"The other incompetent Stan Chilton sucked into this. After you had your little chat with him while he was awaiting transfer to Camp Cupcake west."

"I didn't—"

"You did. You were on the work detail in the yard when he was waiting for the bus. You heard him swearing to get even with Redstone, with Josh. And offered him a way.

Offered him any personal information he needed to get to the woman who'd taken his place. Even though she had nothing to do with taking him down."

"The bitch had it coming," Huntington spat out, giving up the pretense at last.

Tony's grip tightened, and for a brief moment, he truly wondered if he was going to be able to stop himself.

"All right, all right!" Huntington yelped. "I did it. Just back off."

With one of the greatest efforts of his life, Tony released his grip.

"You think this makes any difference to me?" Huntington sneered. "I'll deny all of this. You'll never prove a thing."

"And who's going to believe a convicted felon?"

Huntington paled further; he obviously still hadn't accepted that.

"Besides," Tony went on, "who said anything about proof?"

Huntington blinked then. "What?"

"I told you, I'm not the police. I don't need proof. You're mine now, Huntington. Until I get bored with toying with you. Then I'll decide which of my brothers gets the honor of putting an end to your misery. And believe me, you'll be begging for it long before then."

"But...you got what you wanted!"

It was small of him, perhaps, but Tony took great pleasure in seeing this man's fear escalate to terror. The terror of knowing that all his money, all his social standing, couldn't save him now. It made him smile. That it wasn't a pleasant smile was made evident by the cold sweat that broke out on Huntington's forehead.

"I told you what you wanted to know. Call the guards, the cops, whoever, but leave me the hell alone."

"And where," Tony said in that deadly casual tone, "did you get the idea this was a bargaining session?"

"But I gave you what you wanted." Huntington was whining now. "You have to call them off!"

"I don't have to do a thing. I told you, I have my own rules. And I never promised you a thing, now, did I?"

Pure horror spread over the man's already pale face.

"I don't understand," he whispered, shaking visibly now.

"You never did." With an image in his mind of Lilith facing her worst nightmare, this man, with more courage than this coward had ever dreamed of having, Tony added, "And that will be your fatal mistake."

He left Daniel Huntington a broken, terrified man who would spend his future shaking at every turn, forever looking over his shoulder.

It was almost enough.

Chapter 25

"So it was Daniel all along," Lilith said, feeling more than a little dazed.

"Yes."

Tony's voice was flat, emotionless. As it had been through his entire explanation. She'd heard business reports given with more emotion. Even Liana, who had been in her office when Tony and Josh had arrived, gave him a curious glance. She'd told the young woman to stay; after all, it had been her concern that had started all this in the first place, and it would save Lilith repeating it all later.

Even when Tony had explained what he'd done, what he'd left hanging over her ex-husband's head, he'd shown no sign of anything personal, no hint that this had ever been anything more than a job to him.

Of course, perhaps he couldn't, with his boss standing right there.

Or didn't want to, she thought. Didn't want Josh to know

he'd gotten involved with the woman he was assigned to protect? Or did he not even consider what had happened between them involvement? Was he that casual about sex?

Just because it was life-changing for you…

She pulled herself together, aware Josh was watching her with that steady look that meant his agile mind was pondering, weighing, considering.

"I…thank you." She barely managed to stop herself from saying *Mr. Alvera.* "I appreciate you sticking with this."

When Tony only grimaced, Josh spoke.

"We'll piece together a case that will stand up. He's got good lawyers, but I've got better. He's going to be inside a lot longer than he'd planned," Josh said. "And he's going to be terrified for most of that, thanks to Tony. It's not enough, but…"

"It's enough."

"Sorry for you it was him," Tony said, and for the first time since he'd begun his explanation, emotion crept into his voice. "I know that's not what you wanted to hear."

That jabbed her into a sharper response. "What I *wanted* was to find out who was really behind it. You did that. Thank you," she added again, yanking her voice into a formal, business-like tone; if that's what he wanted, then that's what she'd give him. Apparently he wanted nothing else from her.

Including what she'd already given him.

"Yeah. Great. See you around."

Tony stalked out without another word, so abruptly even Josh looked startled. Her boss, the man who'd given her and everyone at Redstone so much, turned back to her, brows raised in inquiry.

She couldn't do this now. Damn Tony for leaving her to explain. He had to know Josh wouldn't just look the other way after an exit like that.

But she couldn't do it now. She just couldn't.

"Excuse me," she muttered, "I have to…talk to Ian about something. Now."

"Lilith," Josh began.

"Later. Please," she said.

Maybe she could think up a story by then, something he would believe, something close enough to the truth that she wouldn't feel as though she was lying to someone she couldn't bear to lie to.

But as she walked out the door she heard Josh say quietly, "Liana?"

And she heard her assistant, still new enough to Redstone to respond with a formality Josh never required, sigh. "Yes, sir. I think I can explain."

Let her, Lilith thought. It would only be guessing. Although Liana was very perceptive, and didn't miss much. She continued her escape, for one of the few times in her life grateful to have someone else do something she should be doing.

"Wish I could fly you myself," Josh said. "I could use a long stretch in the air, nothing hammering at me but weather or turbulence."

Tony glanced at his boss, who was standing beside him on the tarmac, looking up at the Hawk V, the latest in the Redstone fleet. Tony had seen and heard about the sleek little jet, but hadn't flown on it before. So far only two had been built, and rumors were running rampant that the Hawk V surpassed its nearest competition in range, speed and fuel-efficiency, thanks to Josh's design and Ian Gamble's genius with materials.

"L.A. to Australia, nonstop," Josh said proudly as he ran his gaze over his latest creation. "I wish Elizabeth could see this."

Tony's gaze shot to Josh's face; he rarely spoke about his late wife, and when he did, it wasn't casually. Tony had always known, instinctively, that it was a pain Josh carried deep inside, and he knew enough of such pain himself that he recognized it in this man to whom he owed so much.

"Her family disowned her when she married me," Josh said

quietly. "They ranted about what a mistake she, a Hampton, was making, to throw her future away on a penniless drifter with nothing but a dream to his name."

"Obviously she didn't listen," Tony said, for something to say.

"But I nearly did. All I had to give her was my heart, and I knew she deserved so much better, so much more."

Knowing how it had ended, that his beloved Elizabeth had died after ten short years together, Tony didn't know what to say and his discomfort was growing.

"But she loved me. She swore my heart, my love, was enough. And the day the Hawk I flew for the first time, she was the one who cheered the loudest. She sent her father a photo of the takeoff, the first time she'd communicated with him since she told him she wasn't going to let his ridiculous idea of proper social hierarchy ruin her life."

Tony was utterly speechless now. Josh was looking at him with a quiet understanding that Tony was at a loss to explain.

"Have a good flight," Josh said, and was gone before Tony managed to find his voice.

I could have done without that, he thought as he stared after his boss. It had been unsettling, to say the least. Because, Tony realized, in the entire sixteen years he'd known Josh Redstone, he had never once talked about his late wife like that.

Tony started toward the jet. Obviously, Josh had had a reason. And the only one Tony could think of was the one he most didn't want to think about.

He went up the gangway steps, wondering if Lilith had told Josh about them, if that's why he'd opened up about Elizabeth. He'd obviously been making a point. But the analogy didn't really apply; while Josh might not have had much to recommend him to Elizabeth's patrician parents, he hadn't been starting from negative ground. He might not have been a blue blood, but he hadn't been a gangbanger, either. He hadn't—

Tony stopped dead two steps into the cabin of the jet. Stared. And for the first time in sixteen years, he swore at the man who'd saved him.

"Damn it, Josh!"

Lilith looked up at him, clearly as surprised as he was. "I should have known," she said. But she didn't say it angrily. "When Josh said he needed me to leave in the middle of my work and go to Australia, of all places..."

The gangway slammed shut behind him. A man in the Redstone polo shirt stuck his head out from the cockpit. "Need you to belt in now, folks. We'll be starting to taxi in a moment."

Tony didn't even look at the man. His gaze was fastened on the woman in the luxurious leather reclining seat, with the open, inviting second seat beside her. He knew he had only seconds to decide; if he wanted out, it had to be now, before they started rolling.

She just kept looking at him, and something he saw there in the sea-blue depths of her eyes had him moving to the empty seat and sitting down. Belting in, as instructed. Less than a minute later, the jet began to roll.

"What did he tell you?" she asked softly.

"About Elizabeth. How she went against her upbringing and her parents to marry him. You?"

"He said, 'You've got a fourteen-hour flight. Work it out.' I had no idea what he meant. Until now."

"Work it out," Tony muttered.

"He told me something else," Lilith said slowly. "I didn't realize until just now how he'd meant it. He said sometimes it's better to quit looking at the obstacles and look at the possibilities."

"How do I stop looking at where I came from and where you came from?" he asked, fighting down the hope that was flickering deep down, trying to catch.

She was silent for a moment. Just when he thought she had no answer, either, she said quietly, "Maybe by looking at who you are, and who I am. Now, today. We've both been through some ugly times. We survived."

He couldn't argue with that. "That doesn't change where you came from."

"But it changed where I want to be," she said. "I'm not some perfect, untouchable ice queen."

The memory of her in his arms, crying out as her body convulsed around his, the sweet grip sending him into a fiery explosion unlike anything he'd ever known before, swamped him with fresh heat.

"No," he said, sounding hoarse even to himself. "No, you're not."

As if she'd read his mind, color tinged her cheeks. Her lips parted. Her gaze lowered, but only for a second, as if she had wanted to look away but wouldn't let herself.

And suddenly all the lessons he'd learned, all Josh had taught him about fighting for what he wanted, for never letting others shape—or stop—him, came flooding back.

"And despite that calendar you're so worried about," he said, holding her gaze steadily, "in some ways I'm much, much older than you are."

She didn't flinch. "Yes. In some ways you are. You're also an incurable flirt."

"Was," he said. "I found the cure."

She smiled at that. "I almost believe you."

"Flirting only in the line of duty for me, from now on," he said, meaning it. Then, hesitantly, he went on. "About the other…I know I was out of line. What happened with Lisa, it…"

"Haunts you?"

He didn't like admitting it. "Yes. No matter what anyone says, I will always feel her death was in large part my fault."

"How old were you then?"

He blinked, not sure what that had to do with anything. "It was my first year with security, so…twenty-three."

"Are you the same man you were then?"

He grimaced. "I was a kid."

"If you were in the same situation now, what would you do?"

"Apparently," he said grimly, "I'd tick her off all over again."

"Why did you then?"

"I was too stupid to realize what she'd do."

"So how is it your fault?"

"The law of unintended consequences."

"A harsh law to live by. Didn't one of Merton's causes state that a person's basic values may require certain actions, even if the result is unfavorable?"

His mouth quirked. "We're going to discuss sociology now?"

"It's not what you did, Tony. How you did it, perhaps."

"If this is your way of asking why I didn't learn my lesson, I don't have an answer."

"Maybe it's my way of asking if you're going to keep doing it that way. You can't force someone to do what you want just because you say so," she said. "At least, not anyone with a spine. That's Daniel's way."

"I'm not—" He cut off the fierce protest that he wasn't anything like her ex; they'd been through that before.

"You can, however," Lilith went on, "generally get a reasonable person to do what you want, when it's your area of expertise, and you ask…reasonably."

"How about pleading?" he said, a bit sourly.

He saw one corner of her mouth twitch. "Pleading has its uses."

He steeled himself, knowing it was time, that it was now or never. "It's gut-level, Lilith, to protect someone I love."

He said it purposefully, watching her. She didn't even blink. But she smiled.

"And that's the key, isn't it? I told Liana, just recently, that I try not to get angry with people who care enough to worry about me. I lost sight of that, with you. I think…love got in the way."

He stopped breathing.

"But I do know, really, the difference between wanting to control someone and wanting to keep them safe is love. Just like the difference between resisting it and accepting it is love."

She said it so easily it made his head spin.

"I can't promise I won't make you angry again."

"Oh, I can pretty well guarantee you will. No one said mixing our worlds would be easy. But if Ian and Sam could do it…"

He stared at her, searching for words, wishing that he'd spent less time in his life on the charm and more on the kind of direct honesty this woman required.

"Possibilities, not obstacles, Josh said."

"Yes," she said. "He's built an empire on that principle."

"I love you." He felt a little reckless, blurting it out like that, but reckless seemed in order just now. "I love your nerve, your loyalty, your brains, your grace."

"And I love you," she said, so without hesitation that his heart slammed in his chest. "I love your strength, your determination, your courage and your achievements. And when you take all that and weigh it against the obstacles…"

"They don't matter," he whispered.

"No. What we've found is precious, Tony. Worth fighting for."

"And I'm not one to give up without a fight."

"I know."

"So it can be done. Mixing our worlds."

Lilith gave him a smile that made him shiver in reaction. "We're Redstone. We can do anything."

"Why do I get the feeling Josh expected this?"

Tony laughed, cradling her in his arms. Lilith hovered on the edge of satiated exhaustion; this more than made up for the morning after they hadn't had before.

"Perhaps because the stateroom was fully equipped and prepared?" he suggested.

"It's a Redstone plane. Of course it was."

"Then how about because the usually solicitous and attentive Redstone flight crew vanished after takeoff and we haven't seen or heard them since?"

She laughed. "Now, that I'll believe."

He kissed her, gently, thoroughly, completing her visit to more levels of passion than she'd ever known existed; he had been by turns fierce, ardent, near wild and incredibly gentle, and she loved every one.

"And we," he said with the grin that never failed to make her pulse skip, "still have eight hours to kill."

Lilith knew the obstacles that faced them hadn't vanished. But she also knew that they could be conquered. Especially by two people who had been through fire and come out the stronger for it.

"You were right," Tony said quietly as he nuzzled her ear.

"Of course I was," she teased. "But about what?"

"We're Redstone. We can do anything."

* * * * *

Silhouette Desire kicks off 2009 with
MAN OF THE MONTH, *a yearlong program featuring incredible heroes by stellar authors.*

When navy SEAL Hunter Cabot returns home for some much-needed R & R, he discovers he's a married man. There's just one problem: he's never met his "bride."

Enjoy this sneak peek at Maureen Child's
AN OFFICER AND A MILLIONAIRE.
Available January 2009 from Silhouette Desire.

One

Hunter Cabot, Navy SEAL, had a healing bullet wound in his side, thirty days' leave and, apparently, a wife he'd never met.

On the drive into his hometown of Springville, California, he stopped for gas at Charlie Evans's service station. That's where the trouble started.

"Hunter! Man, it's good to see you! Margie didn't tell us you were coming home."

"Margie?" Hunter leaned back against the front fender of his black pickup truck and winced as his side gave a small twinge of pain. Silently then, he watched as the man he'd known since high school filled his tank.

Charlie grinned, shook his head and pumped gas. "Guess your wife was lookin' for a little 'alone' time with you, huh?"

"My—" Hunter couldn't even say the word. *Wife?* He didn't have a wife. "Look, Charlie..."

"Don't blame her, of course," his friend said with a wink as he finished up and put the gas cap back on. "You being gone all the time with the SEALs must be hard on the ol' love life."

He'd never had any complaints, Hunter thought, frowning at the man still talking a mile a minute. "What're you—"

"Bet Margie's anxious to see you. She told us all about that R & R trip you two took to Bali." Charlie's dark brown eyebrows lifted and wiggled.

"Charlie..."

"Hey, it's okay, you don't have to say a thing, man."

What the hell could he say? Hunter shook his head, paid for his gas and as he left, told himself Charlie was just losing it. Maybe the guy had been smelling gas fumes too long.

But as it turned out, it wasn't just Charlie. Stopped at a red light on Main Street, Hunter glanced out his window to smile at Mrs. Harker, his second-grade teacher who was now at least a hundred years old. In the middle of the crosswalk, the old lady stopped and shouted, "Hunter Cabot, you've got yourself a wonderful wife. I hope you appreciate her."

Scowling now, he only nodded at the old woman—the only teacher who'd ever scared the crap out of him. What the hell was going on here? Was everyone but him nuts?

His temper beginning to boil, he put up with a few more comments about his "wife" on the drive through town before finally pulling into the wide, circular drive leading to the Cabot mansion. Hunter didn't have a clue what was going on, but he planned to get to the bottom of it. Fast.

He grabbed his duffel bag, stalked into the house and paid no attention to the housekeeper, who ran at him, fluttering both hands. "Mr. Hunter!"

"Sorry, Sophie," he called out over his shoulder as he took the stairs two at a time. "Need a shower, then we'll talk."

He marched down the long, carpeted hallway to the rooms that were always kept ready for him. In his suite, Hunter tossed the duffel down and stopped dead. The shower in his bathroom was running. His *wife?*

Anger and curiosity boiled in his gut, creating a churning mass that had him moving forward without even thinking about it. He opened the bathroom door to a wall of steam and the sound of a woman singing—off-key. Margie, no doubt.

Well, if she was his wife...Hunter walked across the room, yanked the shower door open and stared in at a curvy, naked, temptingly wet woman.

She whirled to face him, slapping her arms across her naked body while she gave a short, terrified scream.

Hunter smiled. "Hi, honey. I'm home."

* * * * *

CELEBRATE
60 YEARS
OF PURE READING PLEASURE
WITH **HARLEQUIN®**!

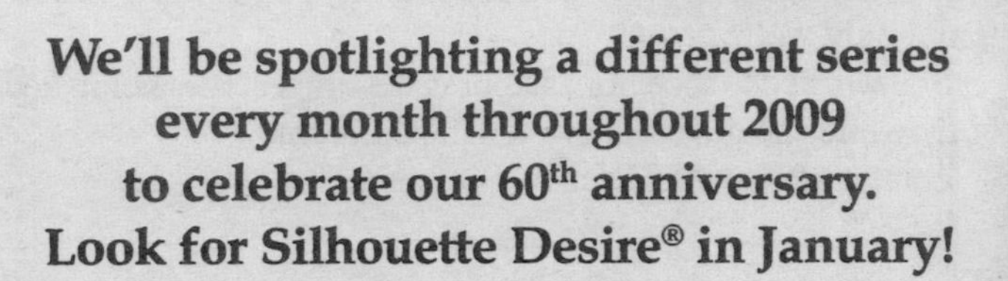

Collect all 12 books in the Silhouette Desire® Man of the Month continuity, starting in January 2009 with *An Officer and a Millionaire* by *USA TODAY* bestselling author Maureen Child.

Look for one new Man of the Month title every month in 2009!

www.eHarlequin.com SDMOMBPA

COMING NEXT MONTH

#1543 BOUNTY HUNTER'S WOMAN—Linda Turner
Broken Arrow Ranch
Hired as her bodyguard, bounty hunter Donovan Jones hasn't even met Priscilla Wyatt before she's kidnapped and he has to rescue her. Priscilla is wary of Donovan's true intentions, but she'll have to learn to put her life—and her heart—in his hands if she wants to save her family's ranch in time.

#1544 BABY'S WATCH—Justine Davis
The Coltons: Family First
Former bad boy Ryder Colton has never felt a connection to much, so he's shocked when he feels one to the baby he helps deliver, as well as her mother. Ana Morales doesn't quite trust this stranger, but when her daughter is taken by a smuggling ring, she teams up with him to rescue the baby. Will they put their lives on the line for love?

#1545 TERMS OF ENGAGEMENT—Kylie Brant
Alpha Squad
On the run from a hit man, Lindsay Bradford's bravery in a hostage situation puts her picture on the news, and now she must flee again. But after they share a passionate night, Detective Jack Langley won't let her go. She never thought she'd trust another cop to help her, but Lindsay finally risks everything when she puts her trust in Jack....

#1546 BURNING SECRETS—Elizabeth Sinclair
When forest ranger Jesse Kingston is sent on forced leave after his best friend dies in a firestorm, he returns home to find himself face-to-face with Karen Ellis—the woman who's carrying his friend's baby. Both suspicious about the man's death, they join together to discover the truth—about the fire and about their hearts' deepest desires.

SRSCNMBPA1208